I0665089

INTRA-COASTAL

ONE YEAR ON ST. PETE BEACH
volume one

A **MONASTRELL** BOOK

ANCHORAGE, AK
2014

INTRA-COASTAL: ONE YEAR ON ST PETE
BEACH Volume One is a work of fiction. Any
resemblance of characters in this work to people
dead, or soon to be dead, is entirely coincidental.

First published as Monastrell 015 in October 2014.

Manufactured in the United States of America.

All Monastrell titles are published for Monastrell
Books by Gene Gregorits.

www.monastrellbooks.com

FIRST PRINTING, October 2014.

Front cover photo: Gene Gregorits
Back cover photo: Gene Gregorits
Book design: Gene Gregorits

"And yet I have known the sea too long to believe in its respect for decency. An elemental force is ruthlessly frank"
— Joseph Conrad, Falk

"The sea, the snotgreen sea, the scrotum-tightening sea."
- James Joyce, Ulysses

"This is the seashore. Neither land nor sea. It's a place that does not exist."
- Alessandro Baricco

"Arresting a single drunk or a single vagrant who has harmed no identifiable person seems unjust, and in a sense it is. But failing to do anything about a score of drunks or a hundred vagrants may destroy an entire community."
- James Q. Wilson

"How do men act on a sinking ship? Do they hold each other? Do they pass around the whisky? Do they cry?"
-Sebastian Junger

INTRA-COASTAL: VOLUME ONE

INTRA-COASTAL

GENE GREGORITS

INTRA-COASTAL: VOLUME ONE

INTRODUCTION

"Now I know why you wanted to get back here so badly. You live in a resort! This is paradise!"

Those were my exact words as I drove across the stretch of causeway that winds its way into St. Pete Beach, Gene's home, Sam's home. The sweeping waterways, the palm trees, the typically Floridian meticulous landscaping, the white buildings touched with pinks and corals and seafoam greens- it all screamed RESORT to me. It IS a resort.

It's also a lot of other things.

Within hours I was introduced to Sam (The Fluffy Cub!), the ne'er do wells and the vagrants and the just regular nice working people that Gene had spoken of so often, sometimes disparagingly but always with a profound affection. I understood right away why he loved this place, and these people. It was seedy, but it was gorgeous.

Some people were there on vacation, others looked retired. But Gene and his friends, they were on vacation from life. They weren't retired, but they sure were retreaded. It took about two hours and a twelve pack before they all started to complain to me behind each other's backs. So much drama! Corey Avenue is the Peyton Place of St. Pete Beach. The tumultuous love affairs, the lost apartments, the snitching. Someone's stash disappeared. Someone walked all the way back from the courthouse up in the city today, barefoot. Someone else tried to sell me his food stamps pennies on the dollar, he needed beer. Another flirted with me relentlessly every time Gene turned his back. "That guy is crazy ya know!" If I really wasn't interested, did I have a sister?

"I hope you have a sister."

They were real dirtbags, a lot of these people. But most of them weren't. Most of them were smart, and they were interesting. Calling themselves "residentially challenged", it was the homeless among them who I ended up having the most in common with. And it was by spending time with them that I realized sometimes having nothing is the only way to have it all. The street. The beach. The sky.

Somehow, when nothing is yours, everything is yours.

-Cynthia Santiglia
Lowell
9.9.14

GREGORITS AND OUTLAW WRITING

There is an adage that says to "write what you know," but to "write what you know" is misleading...What most people know is not very interesting, even if it is what makes them unique and what qualifies writing as fiction and non-fiction, as good and bad. Still this philosophy as a means to produce potentially great art (even though it assumes that everyone is special) is more acceptable than the alternatives. Because few people "know" anything now, students in Creative Writing programs around the world hoping to become the next Stephen Kings or David Foster Wallaces are taught that they don't need to write what they know. They are taught to write novels through news stories and internet investigations. Through observing others through glass. Through biographies of people who are more interesting than they will ever become because they are too busy reading about how the other half lives. There is no need for the "write what you know" novelist to exist when he can live through Lindsay Lohan or Drew Peterson. *Write about someone more interesting than yourself, it's easy an*d *no one will know the difference if you learn technique. It's too dangerous in the real world. There are diseases, drugs, murders, rapes...life.*

Fact: The real writer is an outlaw. Novelists who have helped to define "literature": the Marquis de Sade ejaculating into the wounds of whipped prostitutes, Jean Genet propagating thievery with his tongue buried in other men's assholes, Hubert Selby, Jr spiking his veins all the way to jail, John Rechy selling his dick across the United States, Emile Zola defending Dreyfus successfully against all odds,

William Burroughs shooting his wife in the head, Michel Houellebecq obsessing over sex tourism, James Ellroy breaking and entering to sniff women's panties...These writers know their subjects and they have the skills to convey emotions. In the uber-slick world of Brett Ellis and Augusten Burroughs, as society becomes more intensely boring, privileged and reliant on all things technological, so do its writers. Irvine Welsh has made a mint from writing about heroin addiction, a subject which he admittedly never experienced. Does it matter? Not to the legion of fans who follow Welsh through countless boring novels and even more clichéd descriptions. But the difference between someone like Welsh and William Burroughs or Selby is devastating. Welsh might make you laugh with his amusing anecdotes, but Burroughs and Selby will make you cry. Literature should make you feel. Art versus masturbation.

Enter Gene Gregorits, a self-confessed womanizing, drug-abusing, alcoholic pit-bull-hating self-publishing writer who has had more charges leveled against him than Al Capone. Gregorits clearly writes what he knows. He is hard to love. He makes choices that are difficult to defend. And he often becomes distracted by temptations that life offers. But he's got the chops to back it up and, when he is good, he is very good. One only needs to read both DOG DAYS books to understand. Every printed word is exhaled from Gregorits' blackened lungs. He ticks all the boxes of outlaw auteur and gives hope to renegade writers.

Yes, write what you know. But only if you can and it matters. Jail-time and death are prices to pay for passion. And Gregorits is well aware.

-Alan Hoffman
Chicago, IL
October 2014

A WORLD OF APES

Perhaps the entire gist of INTRA-COASTAL by Gene Gregorits could be summed up in this one line from the book: "You can't do well with intelligence in a world of apes." Obviously this is an over-simplification of the storyline but it is appropriate since Gene is writing about his struggles as a perceptive and intelligent human being trying to survive as best he can being a writer having to take menial jobs to support himself and his beloved cat, Sam, in a world of stupid and/or desperate and insensitive people. The world he describes is the seamier side of St. Petersburg, Florida and environs and the people who inhabit it. It is a kind of guided tour through the decaying Hellscape of modern America and Gene serves it up in full and horrific splendor as only a very talented writer could. Really the only two sympathetic characters in this story are Gene and his cat. The other characters form a gauntlet Gene must navigate through of broken people, crazy people; lost and desperate people. It's like some bizarre accident you can't turn away from and the power of the writing makes it nearly impossible to stop reading. That's a very good thing. Gene knows he doesn't fit in and he seems to have the need to describe what he sees and feels before these people take over the earth. In his words: "it was the age, the post-literary age. . . I was a freak, one of the last, a man stripped of all traces of irony, and I would have had problems anywhere."

I identify completely with that sentiment; and if you do as well you need to read this book. There may not be much time left.

-Skip Slavik, post-literary America, 9/25/14

INTRA-COASTAL: VOLUME ONE

GREGORITS, FLORIDA, & THE KNIFE DICK

As of this writing, I have currently witnessed a feline expire, and have beaten the shit out of my current boss in a dark alley (he was surprisingly cool with it). Florida occupies a strange place in the popular imagination. Those of us of a "certain age" remember "The Disney Sunday Movie", where Florida was the ideal state of being, with our weekly reminder from Michael Eisner, the non-mustachioed head honcho of Disney (Pre-Marvel) who gains the distinction of incurring the wrath of every mustachio-ed animator ever. But anyhoo, Florida was always, in every single one of these movies, revealed to be the ideal state of living everywhere, and if one did not live in similar circumstances, one was a PATHETIC LOSER! Here is the funny thing about American dreams: Americans tend to believe them. Every other civilized country realizes that their national narrative is BULLSHIT, but we have not gotten the memo.

I first met Gene at Danny's Irish Pub, located in Ferndale, Michigan in 2004. At first, I did not like him. He bore a striking resemblance to this born again Christian acid-head taxi driver named GARY, and I did not forgive him for it. 48 hours later, we were on our fifth bottle of wine, smoking crack, and discussing the finer points of post-WW1 era literature. When an organism is evolving to a higher organism, a weird thing happens. This event is called "the evolution of the knife-dick." Gene is one of the few Homo Sapiens that possesses said "knife-dick", one that he has somehow trained as a writing stylus.

Florida used to represent a higher stage of American living, one that has since been degraded to the most retarded examples one can see on Gawker.com. Gene went there, willingly. Detroit was not scuzzy enough for this man. No, he had to go deep into the belly of The Great Whore Of Babylon, unwanted abortion of such that he is, and cut deep into her softer, whiter, underbelly.

With his knife-dick.

- James Schmitt,
  Detroit, 2014

TRAVEL VIA FLOTSAM

Sometimes it's only paradise on the outside. False like a matte painting or a backdrop. You may exist on the same physical plane but you get a different seat in this theater, a different show at a higher price. Paradise is for the tourists, a moving image of palm trees and dunes against blue skies, always living up to expectations. It has to, you see. They only get two weeks off a year. They will this paradise into being with pure need coiling off of their brown steaming lives like tentacles grabbing in all directions. You get to see something different: a horseshoe crab smashed and bleeding blue on the sand. There comes a time when you stop going to the beach.

Before that time comes, you live there. At first it's a dream: the sound of the waves, the strolling out onto the beach naked from your bed because it's three and there's nobody and you start to think like it's your yard. Sure, you have to go to work the next day washing dishes, but that's all OK because you've found a way to snatch your own little slice of paradise pie and you think it's going to be like this forever with the water on your feet and a beer in your hand and full moon on black water and you all alone. So you grab moments of peace each night, take them straight out of the water through your skin, and you tell yourself that's how it is now: peace for you. You keep telling yourself that, even after it's not.

Something bad happens.

Take your pick off the standard menu of very bad things that you do to yourself: choose one. Choose two. Now you can't go back to the house on the beach or you only go back at night after the others are asleep. There are six people living there in the big living room with two tiny chihuahuas that shit all over the floor and nobody ever cleans up the shit but somehow they never step in it either so they know it's there, oh yes, they know. There are bedrooms upstairs but they are not yours and you can't keep any of your stuff that you store in the house from walking away. You sit on the beach all day in the meager shade of a skinny palm feeling acutely the sand in your ass crack and how much time you have to kill, so much time smoking joints and cigarettes with your back to the tree after you broke the only nice thing you had while you were doing too much of the wrong kind of drugs the night before.

It's been raining for forty-five days in a row and there's mold growing on your leather jacket and on all of your shoes and belts.   There's been no work for twelve days   now because of the hurricane. Corey Ave. is starting to look like Pakistan: a giant rift in the middle of the blacktop where it cracked after the sand shifted beneath it.   Water mains spilt, nothing to fill the toilet and no roads in for the trucks to restock the stores. Fistfights breaking out on the hour and nobody's even drunk or smoking any more. Everyone who could leave did, long ago. Last week the National Guard brought in tanks of drinking water and split. They won't be back. Get out now before you get so hungry that the lizards start to look good. You'll have to walk. It's going to be far.

There comes a time when you stop going to the beach. Before that comes another time: the last time you go to the beach. The night you swim out never to come back and instead the ocean steals your will to die, soaks up your poison with its salt. Gives you back a chance you never wanted and dumps you on to shore like a pile of air-bladder seawrack.   So like a schmuck you do it all over again. You get another job. You get healthy. What happened? You were done with this shit. You start to think about other ways to get out. About travel via flotsam: just grab on to whatever floats by.   Whoever floats by.   That can keep you occupied for years. Can make you believe you care.

After a hundred times asking while they silently mock

you with their eyes, going through the formalities but they'll never let you stay because you have *bad vibes,* when you're ready to give up you get lucky and it's a nice place with wooden furniture. You sit down on the edge of the bed and open your suitcase and change into clean clothes and you can't believe you arrived here. You did it by putting one foot in front of another, over and over again. There is something wrong in your body, your strength is low and you are coughing and not getting better, and you should have stopped doing many things long ago. Still you made it here, to this house, a new house far from where you were before, by walking, by force of will. It's all yours, and it's nowhere near the beach, and at night the rain patters down on the broad leaves outside your open window and tree frogs sing, their voices interweaving notes high and low, droning and intermittent. The frogs call so loud and possums hiss from within the bushes, and it's nothing like what you knew before and you feel the breeze on your skin and you are free.

You unpack. There's a book on the table, written by a guy you know, a guy you hung out with, got drunk with.

Crazy wild fucker, but brilliant. No idea where he is now, you last saw him before the hurricane. He told you the book's about everything that happened last year and you've waited to read it till you had a place of your own because it might be about you, or it might be about me.

It might be about how little distance there is between he daydream paradise illusion and the big crack in the street.

Open the cover. Turn the page.

-Jennifer McGrath
Santa Fe, NM
September, 2014

INTRA-COASTAL: VOLUME ONE

GRITZ PORN

What is filth? Merrium-Webster defines filth as: a large and very unpleasant amount of dirt: very dirty conditions or: something that is very offensive or disgusting and often is about sex. While the Oxford dictionary defines filth as: obscene and offensive language or printed material; corrupt behavior: decadence; used as a term of abuse for a person or people one greatly despises; or, albeit in a word: the police. If I have a dirty secret, it is Gene Gregorits. Never since my first encounter with books have I both laughed and felt really bad about it for a good few hours. As in my comparison of dictionaries, Gene strips the grace from any journey into the night and directly neuters hesitancy, fear, and honor. But Gene's is not a type of pornography that is limited to the copulation of clichés nor does it needlessly contain a crescendo of dirt.-- Literature should make you feel much more than you learn. Gene wants to feel his way through the filth of America, today. I promise he will not let you go. If you have made the mistake of reading this forward and not ignoring it as completely worthless, as are all forwards, even those by the authors themselves, I apologize, ahead of time.

-Conor Rickard
New Mexico, September 2014

INTRA-COASTAL: VOLUME ONE

TRUBEE ON GREGORITS

Gene sent me one of his books once, which I absently left on a bus. Hopefully it infected a young, tender mind. Let's assume Gene is real.

Gene stabs to the point, avoiding unnecessary words. He chooses words well to drill home his meaning. He writes of fights and crimes and mental illness and alcoholism and deliberately residing in areas sane people deliberately avoid. He cut off his right earlobe, ate it, and rejoiced in the act to promote one of his books. It would be fun to see Joyce Carol Oates do the same.

The mixed fascination and horror with which I read Gregorits' exploits results from his intentional choice to live contrary to the values with which most of us were brainwashed in our formative years. Gene perpetually drinks, fraternizes with creeps he despises, fights, and rides a hot tank of volcanic rage which colorfully spews forth on his pages. His living conditions marginal, subsisting in crappy jobs, beer in hand (good red wine if he can get some), in perpetual transit from one place to another, one terrible conflict to another, Gene somehow manages to write, WRITE REALLY WELL, and publish and sell books amidst all this madness.

Gene's social function is that of a perpetual outsider looking in at all the rest of us dumb fuckers, incisively explaining to us how we actually appear to his sad, alienated eyes . That is why he must remain outside. If he came inside he would lose this invaluable function for us.

His writings of crimes and transgressions and marginal living and smashing rules and offending social mores possess potent, mostly unacknowledged value and purpose: They are warning signs---"DANGER, DO NOT TRESPASS. HIGH VOLTAGE. LETHAL CONDITIONS AHEAD. OWNER BEARS FIREARMS. TRESPASSERS WILL BE SHOT." Tales of life beyond the edges, beyond staid, comfortable normalcy entertain us and admonish us. Gene ventures past those warning signs to describe in fervid detail what's there. In ancient times cartographers depicted lions and dragons in terra incognita on their maps. Gene lavishes us with engaging accounts of those beasts residing in putrid shitholes where we are far too pussified to venture. Like Christ, Gene has gone to hell and back so we don't have to. Gene would not appreciate that analogy. Jesus would appreciate it even less.

But stop wasting time on my bullshit. Read Gene and decide for yourself.

-John Trubee
September 29, 2014
Santa Rosa, California

INTRA-COASTAL: VOLUME ONE

INTRA-COASTAL: VOLUME ONE

ON THE BEACH

I have not fucked Gene Gregorits.

I just thought you all should know.

But I would be lying if I said I had never thought about it.

Of course I have. I often wonder what it would be like to bang angry, talented misfits. All two of them I am currently aware of, at any rate.

I'm a little picky, too.

I just thought you all should know.

Now that we're better acquainted, I've seen this Ocean City Gene writes of … this "Ocean City of innocent ten year old romantic dreaming, of that Ocean City mystique which was over the years re-affirmed by the accidental melancholy of Madonna's 'Cherish' video or the sandy, sun-baked, salt-water doom in the one for Chris Isaack's 'Wicked Game'." My father took me there. Boardwalk. Hotdog. Books. Beach. Jellyfish. Good memories. From a long time ago.

I have not seen the flip side, the side where Gene dwelt – but like a true traveler I would go, pilgrimage to the wrong side of the sand.

Except Gene knows how to get out alive. I suspect my corpse would wash up on some filthy, sun-dappled cay, half-naked, but with a smile on my face. Don't tell my mother.

Gene's a 21st century poet whether he likes it or not – and I mean that with sincere compliments. Poetry isn't hyming; it's not a fucking haiku; it's not a goddamn sonnet, and while maybe once, poetry embraced those things – poetry now is finding the ugly beautiful.

And then truly understanding the beauty in the ugly – or really, the ugly in the ugly, because it's the only thing that's real. This is what the 21st century has given the best of us.

Gene knows it. I know it.

Do you?
If you don't yet, it's all right. We'll wait for you.
-Dr. Rhonda Baughman
Indianapolis, IN 9-24-14

PORTRAIT OF A MISANTHROPE

Gene's morbidity is exceptionally fertile- he makes it produce humor as well as chills. His nihilism is as brutal and simple as a blow, and by the same token not too convincing. It has no base in philosophy and, being quite bare of shading or qualification, becomes, if taken in overdoses, a trifle tedious. Except for the skeleton grin that creeps over his face when he has devised in fiction some peculiarly grotesque death, Gregorits never deviates into cheerfulness. His rage is unselective. The great skeptics view human nature without admiration but also without ire. Gregorits' misanthropy is too systematic. He is a pessimism machine. He aims to make mincemeat of all civilized humanity,- lawyer and weather forecasters, doctors and detectives, widows and photographers, editors and insurance agents, anarchists and female journalists, men and women. Nevertheless he can and will be read with interest in an age which is getting ready to renounce compromise, kindness, and Christianity.

-Laura Bradford
Lowell, September 2014

THE HISTORY OF INTRA-COASTAL

I.

It is fitting that a novel written by Gene Gregorits has a chaotic, harrowing pre-publication history. In the last year and a half, *Intra-Coastal* has evolved, in erratic leaps and bounds, to become something else entirely than what it was once projected to be.

Dog Days was originally intended to be a single novel, but desperate circumstances led to him splitting it into three shorter novels, so he could publish the material he had already right away as the first volume.

The conditions under which the second volume was written, namely, while locked up in a psychiatric ward, led to that volume being released with a significantly narrower scope, leaving the material which was projected to make up the third volume to become a book unto itself, *Intra-Coastal*, and the material intended for, but not included in the second volume to become the third.

Though the circumstances which lead him to write volume two of *Dog Days* in a psychiatric ward are well known, they call for a brief retelling here. Gene, drunk, and feeling that the sales of *Dog Days Volume One* were not as high as the book deserved, a book he very much believes in, cut off and ate his own earlobe. Of course, he did this on camera and posted it online to drum up sales. He claims to hold the title of having been the first recorded case of autocannibalism in Florida history.

Intra-Coastal was originally envisioned as a substantially longer novel last year, though, after a failed crowd-funding campaign early on, and increasingly bleak and tumultuous times, it is now being released as a trilogy as well.

This, the first volume of his new novel was also, at least partly, written under extreme duress, but this time, the circumstances are a lot more dire. Gene was recently in jail for three weeks. He is currently out on bond, awaiting trial, and could possibly face serious prison time. By the time you read this, there's a chance that he'll already be locked up.

II.

"Everybody likes me here. I've never had so many friends in my entire life. Every five minutes literally there's somebody at my door and they want a beer or a cigarette or just to see what I'm up to. I like that. I've been secretly lonely all my life, and I'm not lonely anymore. It's great."
(On Florida, from an interview published in VICE)

One could have easily gotten the impression that Gene's 'Florida book' was going to be a utopia of sorts, a paradise regained. Filled with drink and drugs and hookers and crime, but a paradise – at least for some – nonetheless. In interviews and online rants, he talked about finally being where he wanted to be, about finally being at home, but utopia is not a place. Literally. Hell is not a real place either, but that doesn't diminish the never ending terror that is other people.

No place lasts as long as its geography suggests. People die from drink and drugs. People get killed, or kill themselves, or die inside. People get locked up.

Neighborhoods die and get developed. What was once beautiful as terra incognita becomes as horrid as the curb crawling crack addict you pass on the corner every night as familiarity sets in. Sometimes you confuse inner space with the outside world and one day you realize that where you thought you were never even existed.

It is an irony of fate that beach might prove to be Gene's ultimate undoing. The reasons why will be made abundantly clear by a simple internet search. Despite the state's lascivious aura, the Florida legal system is as stupid as it is prudish. Remember Mike Diana? What Gene is charged with would not have been a crime in 41 other states, but an arbitrary line drawn in the state's epic of legal fiction threatens to lock him up. Worse, by way of civil commitment, the state reserves the power to do so indefinitely. Florida's seamy underbelly is covered with a clean, white straight-jacket of regressive, draconian law and order, and many never make it out alive.

Sadly, I think that maybe people wouldn't read Gregorits the same way if he were finally allowed a happy ending, but only his most bitter enemies would like to see him locked up in prison. Jack Sargeant once said about Gene's work that "It is through [*his*] madness that we can see beauty." I think that Gene gets this, and that he wouldn't allow it to be otherwise, lest his writing suffer for his lack of suffering.

Gene has referred to *Dog Days* as a "disintegration comedy". Although *Intra-Coastal* has taken on a life of its own, the specter of disintegration is haunting it as well. Disintegration haunts his whole life.

Gene Gregorits is a prophet of disintegration.

-Jordan Gibbons
Canada, October 2014

INTRA-COASTAL: VOLUME ONE

FOREWORD

I was floating around on some other wavelength, I was set out to orbit on speed, crack, heroin, booze, I was geographically ignorant and blisfully lost, and I was absorbing as much as possible: the lingo, the feeling, the same lost-ness which I believe defines the refugee Florida, the Corey Avenue deathtrip. I would hear someone mention the intra-coastal waterway, which has almost nothing to do with this book, which is strictly COASTAL, Gulf coastal. The intra-coastal refers to the vast series of tributaries which flow in off the Gulf; waterfront, yes, but not OUR waterfront. We-the vagrants and walking wounded of Corey Avenue did not drift all the way out to the beach to ignore the beach, no sir: we wanted the goddamn OCEAN.

People, even locals, even natives, call it the "inter-coastal", but if you want to be proper, it's INTRA, man....and if you want to be cute, and malicious, ambitious and seditious, you imply the worst of "intra": intravenous.

I suppose I could have also called it Contra-Coastal. I'm lucky to have anything at all. The chapters which follow, barring the first 4, were written in jail, and I am releasing this book incomplete, as a work-in-progress, out of the same old dire necessity.

There is more to follow. Intra-Coastal Volume One documents my arrival first in St. Pete city, and then on those blood soaked streets that you would probably not even notice upon your own arrival in St. Pete Beach...they are the welcoming party, those people and those structures, those bars, if you come in by bus, or by foot, and of course that was all of us. Pasadena turns into a causeway, and that's the intra-coastal that takes your breath away. Then you hit 75th and Gulf, the ghetto. 75th down to 72nd or so. That's it, a small hell, our hell. But by car? Keep on going, friend. Just keep on going.

And they do, unless it's to buy macrame tourist junk on the east side, the civilized side of that stretch of Gulf Blvd. The other side, though, even sanitized, even broken, even muzzled, is your perfect limbo; that tropical torpor given a proper name and face by men and women who only wanted something beautiful behind them in their narcotized nocturnitis, or in their stubborn embrace of the morning. That end of the world sadness given a proper texture and temper by the deplorable domiciles illegally pardoned by bribed city officials, deep into bad business with bad people. Old Europe, old criminal blood, old Florida corruption: it's the other side of life.

-Gene Gregorits
Miami, FL
50K bond
October 2014

The year previously, I had re-read Cormac McCarthy's Blood Meridian; the thing about it that stuck with me the most was its descriptions of southwestern terrain, those yawning voids its monstrous scalphunters limped through while crazed with thirst or hunger, deranged by rape and murder. My first day alone on the beach, I tried to imagine my every movement, whether it was a certain bus driver I spoke to or a Gatorade bought at an ill-kept liquor store, monitored from afar, the great Judge, the seven foot albino Judge Holden, only a few miles away, able to see me here on this vast coastal plain without any special abilities or tools: the unnaturalness of the landscape, a lunar hell, with nowhere to hide.

INTRA-COASTAL: VOLUME ONE

INTRA-COASTAL

ONE YEAR ON ST PETE BEACH

VOLUME ONE

INTRA-COASTAL: VOLUME ONE

PROLOGUE: NIGHTSWIMMING

It is around midnight when she startles me from my reading: the most beautiful girl I have seen in several hours of wandering the boardwalk, and observing the strolling vacationers from breezy tavern patios. I am in an underground dive bar called Pepper's Tavern, considering the right time to have my historic return to the Atlantic depths. I've been here since around seven, and I've been writing fevered juicehead nonsense on napkins. I've been alternating between my juicehead nonsense and surface talk with strangers on either side of me, talking about Exile on Main Street and the Sex Pistols, about the tavern and about Ocean City. People are more sociable and more inebriated while on vacation. I'm no exception. When I find myself alone, I return to either scribbling or the disintegrating book, Norman Mailer's Pulitzer winner tale of Gary Gilmore's blues. The motel built above our heads is the Sea Scape, one of the cheapest boardwalk-side tourist dives in OC. I remember it well. My mother checked us into a room here on at least four or five occasions. We always seemed to get the same room, I think it was number 19, on the first floor. My mother would gripe about the squalid rooms, she would gripe about being poor. The Sea Scape was never too shabby for my father, and I much preferred it over the three and four star places, long before I knew what went on in the rooms. It wasn't the jaundiced old wino flavor of its economy digs that won me over, but the speediness of check-in and check-out, the narrow hallways, the lack of bellhops and serving trays. In a ritzy place like the Holiday Inn, there were a million things to get caught on between your room and the water. The Sea Scape always gave me the thought that it might as well have been built right in the drink. The Sea Scape was a joke to the other members of my family, but today, I love it more than ever.

Their logo is the same in two thousand seven.

The rooms are the same in two thousand seven.

The more that I think about it, nothing has changed at all...except us.

A lot can happen to a family over so much time...especially a family like mine.

Same logo.
Same rooms.
Same ocean.

In two thousand seven, I have checked in alone, to room number twenty six.

My bag is stashed in there, with my untouched swim shorts.

When I put them on, it will be different than before.

My legs were so pudgy as a kid. I had such fat little legs.

And my hair was more than blonde; in the sun it would go dead white.

The girl leans there to my left and stares at me. The barman comes over, she asks for a vodka cranberry. He asks for I.D. When she speaks, turning on the charm because she hasn't got I.D., I hear a soft girlish voice but with a very hard Russian accent. "State law," the man says. "I'm sorry." With that, he's off to the other end of the bar.

But this Russian girl remains in place, and begins her stare once again.

"You can help me?"

"Me? Can I...no, I'm really sorry. I don't have any I.D. either."

"But they serve you drink? Why they do not ask for card?"

"I don't know."

"How old you are?"

"30. Nearly 31 actually."

"Ah! You do not look theyr-tee!"

She grows silent. When I look back up, I expect her to be gone, but she isn't. Her short black hair contrasts harshly against her skin, which is as pale as mine. I'd guess her age somewhere between 17 and 22, but it's hard to tell in the bar lighting. Her complexion isn't the best, reinforcing my suspicion that she is underage, but a beautiful little thing all the same. She's wearing a raspberry colored mini-skirt and a Mexican-style jacket that only goes halfway to her hips.

"You have girlfriend?"

I nearly choked on my beer. "No, do you have boyfriend?"

"I have friend who is a boy, but I do not have boyfriend."

Just then, the bar man returned. "I hate to interrupt man, but she can't stay here without I.D. State law."

"Okay, I go." The girl glared at the large, barrel chested man and then gave me a similar look. "What is your name?"

"Gene."

"I am Dolly. In room theyr-tee seeks, maybe you come?"

Before I could begin stammering, she was gone. Her purse smacked me on the shoulder on her split second exit-whirl.

"Not bad." The barkeep grinned, and shook his head. "Be careful with those Russian girls. She's probably got a boyfriend waiting for you up there with a stun gun, or a taser or some shit."

"You don't think I should go up there?"

"Fuck no. What ya want for a shot, s'on the house."

I chuckled at the thought of what had just happened. Of course, I had a hard on, and the booze had suddenly gone to my head. I did my shot, went back to my book, and tried to read. I couldn't. I even wrote the door number on my book, just in case.

Maybe she was a cop. With a body like that, it was entrapment if she was. Perhaps she was a highly valuable asset in one of those international live organ smuggling rings. I'd stumble up there with a six pack of Budweiser and a hard on, only to wake up two days later hooked up to an IV in the back of an abandoned Chevy Summit with one or both kidneys removed. No pussy was worth the risk of that, not even this little Slavic siren. And the barkeep had warned me. It was indeed a disapproving expression he wore about ten minutes later, when I called him over to close out my tab and prepare me a take out six of Budweiser.

***

As I left the bar, I stopped to intentionally lose myself, for a moment, in the womblike warmth and magically full bodied life-force of both my condition, and the wild black beyond out there, both deafening and hypnotic. The boardwalk was dead.

Room 36 wasn't hard to find, even though the hallway

was dim then, going on 1 A.M. The roar and hiss of the ocean concealed my footsteps as I approached the second door on the left. I found it unlatched, and pushed it open immediately, before my common sense caught up with me and led me back down the three flights of stairs and to the safety of the bar. There, on a king sized bed, before a large open balcony facing the ocean, laid a half dressed and unshaven young man watching television and smoking a cigarette.

The half nude slob looked up, and mumbled, " 'mon in."

"I'm sorry," came my response, half shouted due to nerves. "I think I have the wrong room."

"She's in the bathroom."

I entered further, stepping gingerly over to a circular, pressed wood card table directly in front of the bed, and sat down, removing a bottle from my brown paper sack.

"I'm Bob," said the thuggish Cossack swine. He had black hair buzzed down close to the scalp, and a significant beer paunch. Would he be the one to perform the surgery? No, I quickly decided. Too young, and evidently he had too little respect for personal hygiene to have any kind of medical know-how. More than likely, he was the muscle of this cloak and dagger outfit. I stepped over to the bed where he seemed to have been rendered temporarily immobile, and shook his hand. "Gene," I told him, holding the mercenary stare of this Russian "Bob". I sat back down and drank my beer. I could feel the ocean wind on my forearms and tried to focus on the blowing curtains until I learned more of this nocturnal scene. In my own grotesque and deviant way, I think I was enjoying myself, if only because this thing, this "Ocean City homecoming / Russian sex fiend slash organ thieves with names suspiciously like American sitcom characters" thing was simply too much to process normally. Then, there was also the twenty or so drinks I was by now radiant with. I could very consciously sense a transformation taking place. The resort town around me was becoming an adult universe, or rather, becoming a part of the greater adult universe around it, the real world, with frightening speed.

Perhaps I was hastening this with my movements, through boardwalk bars and now in this room, instead of the alternate modus operandi, a more traditional day, one in which I simply sat on the beach reading about Gary Gilmore in between vigorous dips in the ocean, perhaps a few pages knocked off in my reporter's notebook, a more civilized attempt to understand what I was doing here. Of course, that's an absurd notion. I'm not wired to behave so delicately. I don't know that I'm wired to really behave at all. I was throwing myself in harm's way, I believe, as a rite of passage. If and when I woke up the next day, there would be no "Ocean City of the mind", no more nineteen eighty-three or nineteen eighty- six or nineteen seventy-nine memories. No place of dreams, no swooning over what might have been out here in my Ocean City of innocent ten year old romantic dreaming, of that Ocean City mystique which was over the years re-affirmed by the accidental melancholy of Madonna's "Cherish" video or the sandy, sun-baked, salt-water doom in the one for Chris Issack's "Wicked Game". Passing mentions of anything I could somehow tie down to Ocean City, transposed feelings, faces, ideas....all that I had inherited as an unreasonably melancholic child and as a dangerously depressed young man would cease to have valid currency here, after tonight. All the things I had absorbed from the world around me, some of them far too deeply, could no longer be so effortlessly fused with the oceanside torpor...the first glance and the last glance, just another vacation...I never wanted to leave. It was becoming clear now, at 1a.m., waiting on a girl in a damp motel room, that a huge part of me never really had. It was time to cut the cord. The booze would help, and so would Bob and Dolly. In the morning, I would have brought these streets, these boardwalk fry stands, these rooms and these waves, all up to date with my new system. With my spunk, with my blood, or both. "You ever have threesome?" Bob muttered, from his station.

"The three of us? Now?"

"Sure, why not? You want?"

"Well, I don't know. I've never done this before, what if I can't get hard?"

"When you see her, you will be hard." The dirty bastard was smiling over there, I could feel it.

The bathroom door opened, and Dolly stepped out, barefoot in a silk see-through nightie. I stood up and placed my left hand down along her right thigh, the other behind her head, and kissed her deeply, with both terror and relief rolling across the surface of my tired and pickled 30 year old skin.

I offered them each a beer from the sack, and stepped out onto the balcony to smoke a cigarette, and think a while. There was nothing to fear in these rooms. Just night people. Nothing to fear down below…just a place where the land meets water.

And Bob was right….I'd never been readier.

***

Dolly sucked us and fucked us proper. But every once in a while, she'd stop and try to convince Bob and I to do something homo, like blow each other.

Bob would narrow his eyes and turn to me, and say, "eh? You want?"

"No….I hope that's alright with you."

Bob would wrinkle his nose up and grin. "Yeh. Not me either."

Neither Bob nor I had any interest in directing the "action" as it were. We simply followed Dolly's instructions. She was clever, and came up with scenarios in which I could quite potentially lose my balance and slip onto Bob's dick (which, I am pleased to report, was not as large as mine), or another in which Bob's dick would graze mine somehow, but we kept outsmarting her. Time and time again, Dolly's impish exhortations to begin cavorting in a homosexual manner were met only with grins from her otherwise agreeable and dutiful servicemen.

Mr. and Mrs. Filthy finally sent me off with their motel room's Gideon-placed bible, after a long bit of sermonizing about the Christian faith. (Dolly: "You are a man who is full of hate. You must not to hate, but to love. You must find favor with man or God will never forgive you.")

When I returned to the bar, it was past closing time but they had forgotten to lock the door. My bartender was cleaning up. "Ah, come on in, what the hell. How'd it go?"

"I had to fuck her with some other fella."

"Ah....that. Yeah, I've been there before."

"They were Christians."

"They....they were what? Christians?"

"Yeah. They gave me this." I held up the bible.

"Je-ZUS Christ. There's some sick fucks in this world, I'll tell ya. I guess you need a drink. Go ahead and tell me more about it, and the whiskey's on the house until I'm ready to head out."

Four A.M. found me on the beach, with another carry-out six of Bud, staring up across the boardwalk courtyard of the Sea Scape Motel. With 20/40 vision, and seeing triple besides, it was impossible to tell if thelone human shape standing on the balcony of the only lit up room on the fourth floor was Bob or Dolly, but I stood and stared back at the shape for some five or ten minutes. The shape never moved, nor did I. Based on what I could remember of that room's placement in the hall, it looked to be dead center.

Room thirty six.

Nobody on the road.

Nobody on the beach.

I removed every last stitch of clothing.

I stripped down quickly, fearing police.

I bent down and buried the six pack in the sand, lifting one out for myself as I finished.

I took it with me, into the great beyond: solid black.

And as I drifted out into all that infinite blackness, almost unbearably electrified from the whiskey and the smells and sounds, it became impossible to tell where the sea ended and the sky began, except to keep my head above, and, of course, my drink. This may have been one of H.P. Lovecraft's fever dreams, and there I was, floating around in it like evil incarnate, destined to vanish forever, into the deep, black sea. Yet still, somehow, I could not shake this fundamental trust in my own innocence, the knawing reminder that I could carve one hell of a hideous path through this life but the worst crime of all would be no worse than stubborn adherence to a religion that wants me more than I want it.

Dreams of a childhood, of a childhood in: This place.

My dreams are the most acute symptom of a virus that wants to make sure I suffer.

A strange peacefulness consumed me, and all other thought was voided.

The water was so very, very warm. And so very, very cold.

Black on black.

I was getting too far from shore.

My beer was just about drained.

A quarter mile offshore, I hurled the bottle out towards Spain, towards France, towards England, and swam back for another.

Like Cthulhu was lashing at my heels.

LAST EXIT TO ST. PETERSBURG

Detective Tim Fontaine, Baltimore P.D., and another detective, a humorless middle-aged female, are staring at me over a metal table with handcuff rings built into it. I am not handcuffed. I have not been arrested. I am cooperating with the police.

For the last three weeks, Detective Fontaine has been investigating me about a knifing incident that I have sworn to them took place in a dark alley just off the 400 block of Lanvale, which I remembered as the location of the shooting of Kima Gregs in the eleventh episode of The Wire's first season.

The truth is that I slashed my own arm open several miles north in Roland Park, with a serrated edge J.A. Henckel's "EverEdge" steak knife - purchased at Macy's in a set of 13 blades that same summer- because my girlfriend was standing in front of the television and refused to move. I'd been trying to watch Ken Burns' documentary about prohibition, the girl was laughing at me, and I had reacted quite badly to her mockery. I nearly bled to death into a black Hefty garbage bag during the ride to the emergency room. I received nearly 50 stitches, in three layers, while flirting aggressively with the nurses there.

The female cop began speaking, during a very impersonal three minutes of the pair making notes on yellow legal pads and looking at me as if I were a streak of feces on the wall. Finally the woman spoke:

"Mr. Gregorits, I am Detective Royer. We need to put this thing to bed now. Detective Fontaine's got real cases to work, and hopefully, we can clear this matter up today before it wastes any more of our time. We're not accusing you of anything, but once a report is filed, we are obligated to investigate. That's how it works, and you have just opened a huge can of worms. Do you understand that?"

"You think I am making this up? Look, I have a flight booked to Florida. I've had an extremely rough couple of years, and I just want to get out of Baltimore and start over. I don't care if you find the guys that attacked me or not. It was just some punk kids!"

"We understand your situation, but we've reviewed all of your statements, and they're just not consistent with the account given to us by Tess Riordan. Nothing adds up here. Anyone who sat and looked at my notes would think you were protecting someone. You can't explain how you contacted Tess after the attack. You can't provide a description of your assailants. After 7 P.M. on, you can't really account for anything concrete. "

"Look. We'd both been drinking. I already explained that I was actually blacked out during much of this. I'm a blackout drunk. I lose large chunks of memory when I drink like I was drinking that night. I remember being attacked on Lanvale, and I remember walking to The Charles Theater to see my co-workers prior to that-"

"Which is why you were in the area, you've said, but Miss Riordan claims that you were with her, at Jerry's Belvedere, all the way up on Old York Road, and-"

"I was there earlier, but she was watching football, and I hate football, so I left, and started drinking. I went to the movies with two bottles of wine, and-"

"You said you saw the movie at 5:15, and you said you had the stub."

"I still have the stub, yeah. Anyway-"

"What was the movie?"

"Drive, with Ryan Gosling. I also had bought a sandwich, a gyro, at the Greek place across the street, that I had for dinner at the movie."

"And then you walked down to North Avenue and wound up on Lanvale."

"I don't even remember the end of the movie. But yeah, I might have taken a bus, but I know I didn't take a cab because I never take cabs, they're expensive."

"In the time frame you've given me here, you couldn't have walked. Vicky, see if you can pull the tapes from that night's 32 bus. So you went back to The Charles. And why again did you go there, to see another movie?"

"No. Again, I worked there for a few years, and I am friends with some of the employees still. I always stop in and say hello."

"Tess made mention that you were also drinking in another bar in Belvedere Square, Swaller At The Holler."

"That must have been a different day. I don't remember going there at all."

"How did you contact Tess from the Lanvale area?"

"I must have asked someone on the street for help. I don't remember."

"We'd check her phone but she claims to have lost it, so we really can't verify anything now."

"Tess is a drunk. She loses her phone all the time."

"Have you considered not drinking so much?"

"I'm working on it."

The detectives sighed and craned their necks and looked at each other. They didn't believe a word of it. I'd been in this situation many times before, but this was the first time that they suspected the female of knifing me. My great fear that night was a stint in the mental hospital, for there is nothing that terrifies me more than captivity. I've been locked up forty or fifty times in my life, and it never gets easier. Fear of incarceration was such that I had willed from myself an impeccably controlled performance, and an explanation for the two and a half inch wound that was sufficient for the doctors, if not for the police. As a concession to political correctness, I never actually identified my fictional attackers as African American, but my moral considerations stopped there.

My great fear on the afternoon of August 27th, during that six hour sweating in Baltimore Street's grimy precinct house, was that Tess would go to jail, and that her brother Rick, a Baltimore homicide cop, would have the charges dropped and come after me.

A week later, another ex of mine persuaded me to see her, using a night of drinking in Fell's Point as bait. Carly seduced me in a men's room, and I woke up many hours later, a few blocks from Lanvale, wi1th my ribs broken, my skull cracked open, and a badly sprained ankle. My wallet was gone, and so was my Army pack, which had been full of books, a computer, and fresh donuts from the Lexington Market. The donuts bothered me most of all.

I wondered if it was the cops who beat me up, tired of my mind games. Tess may have mentioned it to her brother. North Avenue was dangerous, so it may have been a legitimate street mugging. If that's the case, the incident appears karmic in nature.

It doesn't matter now.

My flight was booked for Monday, September 5th, 2011. Without I.D., of course, I'd never be permitted to board the plane.

So Tess drove me to Pennsylvania, where a DMV clerk listened to my sob story and granted me a new photo license.

The next day, Tess drove me and Sam to Baltimore International. Sam's carrier was deemed unacceptable for travel. I remembered that Tess had been drunk when she purchased the thing at a Towson, Maryland Wal-Mart, and had a traffic accident on the way home.

There was a surge of wet, leaden guilt:

Poor Tess.
Poor Sam.

A young woman at the Delta ticket counter found me another carrier for $50. The purchase left me with only 15 and change. But lives can begin anew with fifteen and change.
Mine did.
On St. Pete Beach.

INTRA-COASTAL: VOLUME ONE

FUGITIVES

The rank humidity I encountered in the access corridor of Tampa International airport enveloped me like a fecal sauna. The three hour flight had unsettled Sam, and I was eager to set him free from his plastic carrier. I half-ran directly to baggage claim, and retrieved my duct-taped sack of clothing.

As I turned around toward the exit doors, I found my welcoming party standing there: Tim's sleazeball leather wristbands and Tim's gauche tribal tattoos, Tim's rotten teeth, Tim's greasy grey hair, Tim's acne scars, and Tim's freakishly large belly. Tim had never worked a day in his life, and he was the most horrific caricature of "burnout" that I had ever seen.

We embraced and pretended to be friends. He wore a salt and pepper goatee which announced him, or so he believed, as an artistic man, but rather pronounced his exceptional Hispanic ugliness. It served only to lengthen and sharpen his already long and grotesquely pointed chin.

"Are you shitfaced?" he smirked.

Before I could even respond, before I'd spoken a single word to him in Florida, I already wanted to tear his throat out: standing there with him, in the middle of Tampa fucking International, was Jax, his cowardly and unaltered 10 year old mutt. Sam, already traumatized from the flight, hissed and trembled inside his comfortless carrier.

Feigning obliviousness, or ignorance insofar as Sam was concerned, the homely creep had actually stooped this low to assert his feeble dominance: he'd brought his fucking dog. I had never explicitly asked him to leave the thing at home, assuming that Tim possessed at least that much common sense. I should have known; it was to be the very first in an endless series of cowardly and cringingly desperate power maneuvers on Tim's part; exactly the type of behavior that defined the man, behavior which I now understood had only gotten worse over time.

***

Tim Ramirez considered himself a landmark underground publisher, having bungled his way through the layout design and public release of an undiscerning arts and culture journal called "Esoteric Babies". There had been several issues. He blackmailed family members for booze money and had manipulated several friends back west into springing for his super-premium "Bali Shag" cigarette tobacco, and similarly top-shelf organic dogfood for Jax, who he had always encouraged to defecate as freely as possible on neighbor's lawns, in broad daylight. He spoke only in a faggoty and conceited whisper that no one ever wanted to hear; it was blasted by too many years of sloth and fear and dope.

Tim Ramirez was the most treacherous, most toxic man I'd ever met, a dangerously jealous and helpless man; it was those qualities, and the depth to which he was both aware of them and imprisoned by them, that made him dangerous. He'd latched onto me after a chance meeting in a Los Angeles bar that I had zero recollection of. Being a man who specialized in bartering with the goods of others, it didn't take much to arouse his interest: cash, a car, a drug connection, a literary association, or even a bar tab. In my case, it was a famous girlfriend. I had a tendency to spout off about her at that time; we were splitting up and I wanted everyone to know that. Tim would size up a man's holdings almost as if by osmosis, and immediately the beady eyed sociopath would begin organizing the transfer of the material, or the information he had verified. You'd invite Tim over for drinks, and by the next day, you'd be neck-deep in a deal with man you'd never heard of, under terms you didn't remember agreeing to; a deal which benefited only your new pal Tim Ramirez. Mr. Moocho Rising.

Over the years, I'd always kept him at arm's length, ignoring his constant suggestions that I move out west to share an apartment with him in Chico, CA. It was obvious to me from the very beginning that Jim was mortally petrified of work. He had been honing his sociopathic instincts, and avoiding common sacrifices for so long that his serial mooching had become nearly effortless to him. And much to the horror of his victims, Tim -as with any genuine mooch- was completely shameless. Tim's face itself had shifted over the years: the sloth and the flimsy excuses and the lying had given him a sleepy appearance. He was "over-underworked." His eyes drooped and betrayed blatantly in them was a nauseating look of guilt, but Tim's sleepy, guilty eyes were both of them thoroughly manufactured things, for he got plenty of sleep (Tim was strictly nocturnal, so as not to get in the way of the working people around him) and the false shame, worn for so many years to incite pity, had simply taken over: a permanent "mooch mug". In ten years, I knew better than to mention work to Tim. If you made even the slightest implication of moochery to him, Sensitive Whispering Tim would shatter and explode right where he sat (or, in a rare moment, where he stood) and be replaced by Violent Humiliated Tim.

As woundingly obscene as it was to witness Violent Humiliated Tim Ramirez, this side of him did -if only fleetingly- earn the implications of his ridiculous forearm tattoos and leather wristbands, which otherwise, much like his deliberate and determined flatulence, only highlighted a crazed urgency to mask his multifaceted impotence in any masculine facade available to him, such as philosophical banter.

Tim proclaimed himself relentlessly to all within earshot to be a philosopher, prizing only the weakest or loneliest individuals from the world around him; these people he would try to establish as his constituency...druggy old dwarves, hirsute barmaids, sleazy lawyers, petty crooks, and failed musicians like Tim himself.

No genuine literary sort would willingly break bread with the fraudulent cretin, and I was no exception. In Detroit, in Baltimore, for years and years, I ignored Tim's 3 and 4 and 5 A.M. phone calls, which he made at a disturbing regularity despite my pleas to him.

Me: "Tim, I have to work."

Tim: "What do you know about work? I work!"

Me: "You do not work, Tim. You have never worked."

Tim: "Fuck you motherfucker! You can't even drive a car!"

Tim's pickup truck had been given to him by someone, and he believed that this also was proof of his virility.

Tim fancied brotherly ribbing to be a sign of exalted machismo, so he indulged in it frequently, but it was to remain very one sided. You could not get personal with Sleepy Hungry Ashamed Lonely Tim. In dealing with him, I regarded him very much as a menstruating schizophrenic woman on speed: kid gloves, in other words. That's what Tim demanded of all those around him.

"Geeeeeeene,", he would begin, while sucking on a joint stoically, "you don't understaaaaaaaaand....I went to HAR-verrrrrrrd, and I'm a phi-LOS-o-pherrrrrrr, Geeeeeene....I'm not going to wash DISH-es like youuuuuu, Geeeeeene, I'm not like youuuuuu...and I have a HER-niaaaaaah, Geeeeene, I have HEALTH problems.... You should try to learrrrrrn from me, I could make you a better WRI-derrrrr, Geeeene....you're not egreeeeeeee-gious, Gene, but you're just not graaaaaaaaa-cious...."

***

I was appalled and furious, doing my best to contain myself as Tim's dog –which was nearly as big as me- repeatedly broke wind in my face and bruised my testicles with its paws while trying to walk in a circle inside the truck's cab. Sam recoiled in misery below, between my ankles, as we began the 45 minute drive from Tampa International to St. Pete.

In its idiotic enthusiasm, the shaggy gray and black dog smacked me in the face over 20 times with its tail, and Tim continued to say nothing about it, while brazenly powering the grotesquely oversized pickup truck over the Tampa Bay highway. "Jax", he would mutter, absently, intentionally failing to influence the dog's vile behavior. I ground my teeth and moaned in rage as Tim briefed me on the night's agendas. Finally, as he was handrolling one of his Bali Shag cigarettes, steering with his knees in a self-conscious attempt to look cool, I had to say something to him.

"God DAMMIT! Look, I just had a really rough flight with Sam, and Sam is not doing well either, flying is very hard on cats, would you PLEASE? The dog?" "Jax!" This time he was audible to the subnormal beast, and it retreated into the narrow space behind the driver's seat, panting and groaning like a hypersexual mongoloid. The bay was several miles wide, engulfing us: I recalled this stretch of road from my wasted bus trip all those years ago. I started hoping that the shock of all that dark water would remain as exciting to me.

With the mutt momentarily keeping its snout and stabbing paws out of the general area of my dick, Sam leapt to my lap, out of his carrier, and stood on his hind legs, bracing himself against the glass of the driver's side window with his paws. He began licking his lips and furrowing his brow, deeply unhappy with the whole situation.

I was desperate to calm my nerves with the first drink of the night, and to get Sam sorted out at the house. I was delirious when we arrived. All shadows, strange smells, someone's home. I hadn't had a proper home in 3 or 4 years.

An American flag hung half-mast above the low front stoop. It was a blue, two story affair, quite pleasant, really, if middle class excess is really your bag; well-furnished but noticeably unclean, quite sickeningly so, with large dust motes and clumps of sticky dog hair co-mingling along the grimy baseboards. Tim, altogether devoid of irony, stated to me at that exact moment: "Geeeeeeene, it was part of an agreement between me and Johhhhhn that I have to clean the houuuuuuuse, so don't make any fucking messssssses, okaaaaay? You've got to help me cleeeeeeeean."

An expensive leather sofa dominated the living room along with a high end digital stereo receiver, a plasma TV, a small redwood bar which was obliterated by layers of dust. The bottles were all empty. My first impression, even in my debilitated state, was that a lot of effort had gone to presenting an image of swank bachelorhood, a kind of Details Magazine cool.

We made our way to the bar.

ROUTINE ONE

Sam was soon spending his days lounging in the red tanbark which comprised the whole of John's front yard, with ferns and several flowering bushes. Each day I woke to that feeling one had as a child when summer hits, the shock of a new routine, a new kindness...the giddiness of hot breezes and that kid-frenzy released by chlorinated water and hot sun and lemonade and murmurings of parents and relatives who would always be there, and of course the freedom of weightlessness. I knew that in my obscene tropical paradise there would be old worries and old agonies for a short while longer, but even these would be filtered through a new lens, a sun bleached "none of this is real" lens, and Sam had all the lizards in the world for his own yellow eyes to chase.

I would find myself walking from 8th Avenue down to Central, the tawdry and synthetic main drag, the division between north and south St Pete, exploring the rancid alleyways and the posh Tampa Bay waterfront, hellbent on finding work. I completed nearly a hundred applications, dismally and angrily. Chinese take-out food was a distant memory, a symbol of better times. I was lucky to have eggs and potatoes back in John's kitchen.

Men's Health Magazine had just ranked St. Pete as "the saddest city in America", and Creative Loafing, the region's sterilized and lobotomized alternative weekly paper, was fairly up in arms about the designation. Apparently, this finding had been based on the city's skyrocketing suicide and mental illness rates, and during my explorations, I observed an overwhelming contextualization of the Men's Health claim: the tropical urban squalor was epic in scale. I began to resign myself to it all. My new home was a frightening mixture of pulverizing poverty, of aggressive spiritual heaviness, of physical degradation, of weather beaten inertia.

Half of downtown's buildings seemed to be flophouses, where the befouled bodies of scourged men could be seen lounging in the stagnant afternoons, chain smoking their one dollar packs of "little cigars". I later learned that these ersatz smokes were comprised of only 50% tobacco. The other 50% was -is- unknown, but from the looks of St. Pete's walking wounded, it wasn't fit for human consumption. Ancient air conditions gone crimson with rust sat in the 2nd, 3rd, 4th, 5th story windows of flophouses staining the gruesome old cinderblock and stucco walls with dark waterstains that smelled of body odor and nicotine and death. There were dirty yellow awnings that had been painted decades ago with names like The Seville, or The Dalton, or The Tropical Arms. The lopsided and sinking palatial library, situated on Mirror Lake, became a regular destination for me. I would drag myself in there after a day of filling out job applications, eager for the body shock of air conditioning, and cold water. Bums were sleeping in its various alcoves and on all the benches. The library stunk of shit and booze. But it was quiet. Next door sat the Social Services building where hordes of poor blacks and and whites would congregate, chain smoking out front, lining up in the various offices for free food, free money, or free housing. I applied for food stamps there and while I turned my back to pick up my army bag, a black war veteran standing in line behind me snatched my ten dollar cellphone off the clerk's counter. He stared at me defiantly, pink keloid scars roaming from his nose down to his chin.

The sad, dreamy Mirror Lake area was a haven for vagrants and drug addicts of all sizes, shapes, and colors. Stretching a solid mile and a half around, you couldn't deny the beauty of the lake itself, and I would spend the odd hour there pretending to be homeless and rapping with hustlers, fantasizing about cool shady bars, and crack whore sex, and Chinese lunch buffets, and anything else a penniless man imagines for himself.

For the first time in so long I was in a position to allow myself a free-range kind of personal investment, a concentrated interaction with my surroundings; I'd been seeing the same things over and over again, the same places, the only real difference being the physical disintegration of acquaintances...the gradual liberation of memories over time, memories that I never wanted in the first place.

Here in Florida, it was if I had woken up on another planet, a place that was detached in every way from all other places, and its specialness was reaffirmed everywhere I looked; in my periphery, always, whether passing through a sandy vacant lot, down an alley, through the open air drug market known as Williams Park, were lizards of a startling variety: Mediterranean geckos, tropical house geckos, brown anoles, green anoles, knight anoles, racerunners...billions of omnipresent beasts ranging in size from 3 to 12 inches, and on a bright 95 degree day, I would walk for hours just to enjoy the sight of them darting across sunbaked shelves of sidewalk, with a stealth and agility that made me feel like Bobo the Dancing Bear. Before inevitably spooking a lizard into shelter, it was impossible not to stop and stare, contemplating them and their disconcerting spasms and tics, with a little brown anole's head and most of its body alternating between two different frozen poses, back and forth, like a strange little machine, short-circuiting there without any sound at all.

INTRA-COASTAL: VOLUME ONE

LOST BOYS

For too many years, it had been this way, either incapable of responsibility, or incapable of telling myself otherwise. Whereas others found their place in commerce, I found mine in art which is a very sanitary way of saying that my true talent was in maintaining that spark of awe (and dread), awe at the cosmic awfulness and ecstasy of everything. That had nothing to do, my coming to St. Pete., with Kerouac, because Kerouac's transition to Florida was his dying, first and foremost, moving ahead of his living. It was the opposite with me, although I am not sure that standing has remained. But it was Kerouac that got me going: in the dark of my youngest years as a reader, it was Kerouac that set me free, set me to being ecstatic at what I was naturally so lurching, lunging towards.

Of course, always caught in that irreconcilable bind between elation and nausea and terror in the wake of each and any newfound self-revelation or reflection, I came to understand that what THEY lacked, I naturally produced in abundance, like the teeth of a rat which will never stop growing. I had to chew up the scenery. I had to consume everything that got in my way. And anyone who entered my drowning life would soon flee in mortification upon realizing the penalties, the strain, and the violence...of me.

It was too late to start explaining: you either got it or you didn't.

Tim got it: too well.

John was a sissy and simply scared shitless of me, both because and in spite of my intelligence.

And old Dan...he was hard to read. I got the impression that Dan didn't really LIKE anyone, but he got lonely, without women…chances were, Dan was just happy to have someone to drink beer with on occasion.

The first days passed quickly and then, after 2 or 3 weeks, I started to worry that I'd never find a new job.

St. Petersburg, the yuppie St. Petersburg, anyway, was exotic banality, all the way: it was a kind of middle class, sub-West Palm Beach milquetoast decadence. There were real estate moguls paired with porn actors, slumming lawyers dabbling in poetry and acrylic paint, and worst of all, the ubiquitous zomboid hipster population…it was white, white, white. Only the black junkies and the white junkies seemed to know, the hustlers were the only ones who knew, how to fucking really ENJOY this Florida beauty. I kept to them, during week 3, week 4, week 5, jobless, hungry, roaming.

From the pastel perversity of the Old Northeast, in the sticky sweet film which filtered down from the boughs of these menacing Florida trees, the names of which I never knew, and all that money, and that sharp stagnation which clung snugly to each spooky breeze rolling off wretched Tampa Bay, I rode the 32 bus northwest towards 59th Street; I took in the sights. Waterfront duplexes and apartment houses became mansions with boathouses, the Bay glittering through the tinted plexiglass of the Pinellas-Suncoast Transit Authority windows, I saw geogeous stone arch bridges in 100 foot spans which led to a commercial sector, a hilarious 4-hour XXX gang bang of multiplex cinemas, supermarkets, discount drug stores, salons, gyms, take out restaurants, and corporate car maintenance centers. These banal churches around me were warming to me, don't misunderstand, especially on that first morning, experiencing the 32 bus in all my hangover hypersensitivity and dislocated delirium, collectively magical, it was…a kind of cordon between me and the brutarian wilds which must surely exist beyond, the places I had found myself in, in every city: crackhouses. Trailer parks. Bad motels.

Another mile then left me on 59th Street, bordering on Pinellas Park which had been frequently described to me as an un-survivable green inferno of white trash incest and violence. The biggest in the state of Florida. Something about screwing young retrograde Florida crackers with names like Brit and Bree and Jenn and Shelly, well...there's the badness that I want, and the badness that I EXPECT myself to want, and that comes from OTHER people, with other ideas...maybe I'd lost sight of which was which, but passing a trailer park, I could only imagine super-hot 4 day meth sex with skanks who knew –really KNEW- how to suck cock. Pardon me.

I stepped off the bus at an intersection and made my way a hundred yards in this direction, then that. Running about 30 minutes early, and being in such an alien place, I allowed myself a little wanderlust, and I sweltered calmly in that 100 degree day. Oh, yes...I understand now, as I did then, why people have such unreserved loathing for Florida. And I also understand now, as I did then, why I could never share in it. Florida is many things, but it is not BORING and it is not EASY. The ground I walked on was a swamp of 4-LOKO cans, glassine bags, empty cigarette packs, and Winn Dixie shopping bags. I LIKED that, you see. There stood around me a thriving Citgo station, a tire shop, a particularly Satanic-looking row of decrepit bungalows, and a used bookstore, which looked to have been abandoned for over 20 years. "Thank GOD," I said to myself, wishing fervently for the closure of all other bookstores. I'd come to hate everything and anything even vaguely literary; I preferred to buy books on Amazon. As far as I was concerned, literary America was dead, especially the bookstores, because they'd never reached out to anyone: afraid of working people, they stagnated, they inbred, they sucked each other off, they   BLURBED EACH OTHER TO DEATH, until they couldn't stand looking at one another anymore, at which point what little remained had to also whither and die. Spanish moss was huge out here in these open areas, weeping willows and occasionally a weirdo palm. Hell! It was Hell and I loved it!

Although my destination was Reese Builders, where I was to interview for a job selling windows, it occurred to me that I'd become weak with hunger, and so I advanced towards an overpass 3 blocks north. My bus had come to a stop there –I knew it was the same bus because the driver was exiting with a broken nose while other violence seemed to be exploding on board. A Burger King sign loomed in the distance. I left the bus behind, and entered the overpass, flipping open my phone. This was indeed my very first cellphone, purchased for me by my mother the day before; it was a little flip phone that could take photos. The phone told me the time: 5 minutes past 4. I had 25 minutes to get there. Through the slimy tunnel, I could feel beings, see shapes, moving around me in the dark: homeless men.

In the Burger King, I ordered in a hurry, gobbling a Whopper Jr. through the tunnel and back to the intersection of 59th and 22nd. Being only six blocks from the stop, I assumed the distance to my interview would be minimal, and the clock now read 4:14. But the connecting road was known as "Industrial Drive", and not even technically PART of 59th St: this was a brand NEW netherworld, and it was industrial alright. A mortifying stench fairly ejaculated from a pair of lavatorial canals, drainage ditches I suppose, which lined either side of that sullen, putrid road. Stark roominghouses and bungalows loomed there like sad old monsters in the wet dusk.

Each of Industrial Road's blocks were a quarter mile long and it was nearly 4:30. I had a mile to 22nd, and then the length from Industrial Road to the front door of Reece which could be another mile or more. Had I misjudged all of this deliberately?

I was wearing tan slacks and a button down blue shirt which had now turned purple with sweat. I took off at a full run towards 22nd, barely noticing the inhabitants of the area staring at me from beach chairs, drinking Hurricane High Gravity Lager, stoically bearing witness to all of the mutant beasts eating the sewage of Joe's Creek, which was apparently the official name of the entire neighborhood. The creek proper was the most vile flow of liquid I'd seen since I'd run over a dead rat with a stolen ten-speed one rancid NYC summer ten years ago.

I passed boat storage garages, dry docks I suppose you'd call them...size of grain mills.....4 drunks hid under the Joe's Creek bridge with homemade fishing poles...sepia toned liquor stores...so many drunks and dirty egrets, great blue herons, all co-mingling peacefully...

By 4:40, I had to rest. I'd reached 21st Avenue, and could see then, there in the belly of the beast, what a fearsome, apocalyptic "industrial park" it truly was. I imagined being thrown into Joe's Creek and getting my fingertips perforated by needles and razor blades in mid-breaststroke, choking on the lethal elements, the price of doing business; repo offices and fish processing centers, distribution centers, chemical factories, body shops...the stench of fish guts walloped me in the late afternoon heat. I didn't want to consider the condition of my once clean blue shirt, nor my handshake. At least my hangover was gone now, kind of.

It was 4:50, and if I hadn't blown the interview already, I surely would if I stood out there another ten minutes trying to cool off, which couldn't occur anyway as it was only growing hotter. I remember this day as being a Wednesday, a fecal Florida Wednesday of nightmares and heat and general punishment. I must have harkened back to my years -3,4,5, maybe 6?- lost drunk in the hideous post-industrial fuck-me-in-the-ass suburbs of Detroit: I was making $6 an hour at Border's Books. This job, I thought, could never be so terrible. At least it stank. Borders didn't even SMELL like anything.

REECE

The air conditioning in the pressed wood appointed and fiberglass windowed front office was an ice-bath; I became taciturn with the epidermal trauma. I let an orgasmic sigh escape my lips which were pursed with DT grimness. The middle aged blond Reece had employed as a secretary stared me down, her mouth agape, un-amused.

"Sorry," I lisped. "I'm...uh...Gene, you know? Justin?"

"Mr...*Gregor...tis*...from...4:30?"

"I know, I got lost, I'm sorry."

"Aaaaaand.....I take it you don't have a CAR."

"The ad said..."

"Let me get Paul on the line..."

Her right shoulder shot up into her creamy neck as she handed me a clipboard, with one hand to steady the phone, and dug around in her desk for a pen with the other. Extending it over the desk, she eye-fucked me again, total incredulity, or maybe something else?

"Take a seat and fill that out. If he's gone for the day, I'll...Paul? Justin...Grag...Gray-grotis? From 4:30? Yes. Well...I...he's HERE.Okay?"

I watched her hang up the phone, then stared down at the form which was identical to the 20 or 30 thousand other ones I had filled out in recent years? I knew I wouldn't get the job. I never got the job. But the cruel truth was that if I kept going...40,000 applications, 50,000 applications, I'd make it, and I'd be crazier then. I'd be more alcoholic. More suicidal. I'd be less capable of actually HOLDING a job with each new one I was for some perverse reason actually given. I thought of Sam, and, for the millionth time, how much easier my life would be without him. My skin had gone cold. To the left of me was a bubble gum machine, rubber plants, magazines, all that shit. It was a shithole. I was shit. Everything was shit.

I felt vibrations then, and tensed up, expecting the next blast of shit, when the room erupted with an explosion of gracelessness, a swirl of idiot motion and directionless energy and meaningless volume. Here was Paul, a fat fuck moron, and he had launched himself into that front office with everything to prove and nothing at his disposal to prove it with. He didn't even know why he existed, the repulsive fat fuck, and I wished I could cut this man's throat right then and there. I'd simply kill the fat man, rape the arrogant secretary, and leave the whole place behind me in flames. Maybe the entire toxic nightmare "industrial park" would go up with it.

The fat man stood lurching above me, all 10th rate crazyman shtick, an overcompensatory boob with buck teeth, short cropped blonde hair, and cheap white-trash jewelry.

He was looking at his watch.

"Ooooooooh kaaaaaaay," he said in a grossly feminine manner. "Not cooooool. Why should I see you a whole half hour late, hmmmmmm? I mean, who DOES that?"

I found myself exactly then fervently hoping that Paul took the first opportune time to identify himself as a homosexual, because if THAT guy was straight, and if he had both money and pussy while I floundered in this way, I'd simply have to find a way to kill Sam and I.

He was the most repulsive man I'd ever met, besides Tim Ramirez. No...I take that back: Paul was worse. Now that I think about it –I am writing this from St Pete proper, less than a mile from that old office- it would make a lot of sense to disguise myself and beat Paul into an emergency room tonight, three years later....I'm drinking....back to the story....

"I'm sorry, I got lost. I just moved to Florida, and I'm still getting the bus system and the geography figured out."

"The geography? It's a grid system. You don't understand a grid? And there are schedules for the buses which tell you the time! You can't tell time?" I stared into his chest, his tits. For some reason I fantasized about those tits as woman's tits, then I thought about stabbing him in the face.

Paul wrinkled up his flushed Baby Huey countenance, and shook it spasmodically: "yeaaaaaah....just...don't. You're already here so let's just DO this *thaaaaaaang*."

At that moment Paul broke into some kind of Negroidal club dance that made me want to curl up and die all over again. "Nancy," he said, continuing his passive aggressive locomotion, head bobbing to some invisible Britney Spears video in an onanistic moment of barren, incoherent sarcasm: "I'll be staying late for Mr. Gray-graht-its, Graygrotis here."

"Gregorits."

"Excuse me?"

"It's...just Gregorits. No double consonants, nothing like that. You just sound it out, you know, phonetically, and you got it."

"Wow," he said.

The world had been making me feel small since I was able to *show* weakness. Anyone could bully me. And in not harming people, I could not tell if I was losing my soul or just barely holding onto it.

Paul led me to an adjacent room which held a folding card table and a pair of folding plastic chairs. There was a water cooler, a sales board, cheap carpet, the terrible reek of Maxwell House made in a 20 year old Mr. Coffee which had never been cleaned: all good signs that your life is over. End of the road desperation looks like this.

"Do you have sales experience?"

"Yes. I ran my own eBay business for 6 years. I handled every aspect of it including the customers, and…"

"Justin, Justin, listen…"

"Uh, Gene please."

"Excuse me? I thought-"

"I go by my middle name, like a lot of people."

"Okay, I see you're already complicating things. I ask you for sales experience and give me mail order, and…"

"No, it was more than mail order. I had to develop my own product, my own clientele, and my own facility. It was-"

"Are you done?"

"Sure."

The dancing pig man looked at his watch. "Look, the phone job is taken. What I have is appointment setting. And you have no sales background, but everyone else I hire for appointment setting is green. We work the streets, all over this part of the state, not just Pinellas County, but Hillsborough….all over. You knock at prospective homes, you pitch the script, you get our people in there for demonstrations. The commission's good. It's a competitive environment and we have good people here, and some of them are making serious money. That's it. That sound like something you'd be interested in?

"Absolutely, but I don't have a car."

"You don't have a license?"

"No, I mean, I don't *drive*."

"You don't *drive*?"

"No."

"Why do you not *drive*?"

"I grew up in New York, with the trains. Never drove, you know."

"My cousins live in Brooklyn. They have cars."

"Well, I don't drive."

"Ok, whatever. We use a van. We all take the same van out every day, 4-crew, 5-crew, sometimes less if we're training new people. I give you a zone, you work that zone, you cover it. We all cover our own streets. Then we reconvene for lunch, then again to go home. We work Tuesday through Saturday. You have any felonies?"

"No."

"Anything? We check!"

"Misdemeanor assault, ten years ago. Just a barfight. Probably wouldn't even come up."

"Okay. We'll start you Tuesday. You'll need khakis, or khaki shorts. I recommend shorts. And good walking shoes. That's VERY important. This job is 2 things: getting the script down, and walking. Take the application with you and fill it out, and bring it back. 9 A.M. You need a phone, too, I forgot all about that. You do have a phone right?"

"I am proud to say that I am for the first time in my life the owner of a cellular telephone."

"You're kidding."

"No, just got it, and I have it all figured out so the phone thing is NOT a problem."

"Please don't make me regret this. I won't ask about your arms, but please try to keep them halfway covered."

We shook hands and I was ecstatic to have a job, positively elated, even if it was a low-rent door to door geek show of a job. The afternoon blaze had diminished slightly and the churning, throbbing hum of the industrial park was gone as if spooked away by my approaching footfalls. In the distance, on Industrial Drive, I could see the toxic waste fishermen emerging topside from their sordid sojourn in the belly of Joe's Creek, like a gateway to Lake LaJeune, the biggest toxic waste cesspool in the world, someone had told me. They were all smiling over their day's catch of freak fish.

There was a biker bar there at the end of 22nd, which I ducked into, hoping to celebrate my good fortune with one of their $1 Michelob Ultra-Lite mugs which they advertised over the front door. The inevitable cigarettes and forced optimism, the stringent denial, the Kid Rock on the jukebox. An old woman gave me a ghostly and melancholy smile. Another old woman played a trivia game with a senile French Bulldog on her lap. A malevolent little meth head leering at Miley Cyrus on the bar TV, in monotone administering His Final Judgment:

"I'd suck the corn out of her shit."

My laugh gave me goosebumps, it pierced through my shambolic meditation process and it left me vulnerable like that, vulnerable to communication. I'd have to engage.

The meth head was leering at ME.

The barmaid put a small mug down in front of me. "Just ignore him," she implored. "He's harmless. That'll be a dollar, honey. RON, KNOCK IT OFF."

I put a 5 down on the bar, stashing a few remaining singles in my back pocket. Bus fare.

Kid Rock ended. I knocked back the cold, worthless beer, ordered another.

Ron looked straight at me.

"You dig girls, man? You a fucking faggot? Miley Cyrus, what do you think she is, 12? If I fucked her in the ass, I'd break my fuckin back tryin to suck the shit off my dick. What do you think of that?"

I looked at him. I just sat there and looked.

It was dark when I left the bar: dreamlike, the cicadas roaring. I told myself it was dreamlike and beautiful, stopping off at a phosphorescent "Snak Shak" for a can of Hurricane High Gravity Lager.

The intersection's traffic lights burned green 2 blocks up. Shades of black bleeding into one another, obscuring movements.

Not dreamlike.

It was all waking evil.

INTRA-COASTAL: VOLUME ONE

OLD N.E.

There was the whole weekend, *and* Monday, to enjoy before my sales career would begin, and with that, a great trepidation: between my propensity for drama and the genuineness of my attraction to ocean energy, I knew that my first glimpse of the Gulf of Mexico would likely set off a few violent brain spasms. I'd been biding my time, and even stashed away $20 for wine and bus fare. I was ready to go to pieces before it all.

John was very happy to hear the good news, his bloodshot Scandinavian party-boy blues conveying nothing more than sexual coke panic, but happy nonetheless.

"See, I told ya buddy. Look man, you're gonna do great. We'll go out tonight and celebrate, ok?"

John's fiance, Laura, seemed to me the drippiest tart in all of Central Florida. An Amazonian Italian blonde with a bulbous honker, she was neck deep in denial over the severity of John's raging stimulant abuse. Her shallow and spineless nature shielded her rigid, expectant, and commodious mind from the explicit barrage of evidence all around her: rapid speech, frequent dashing out, violent mood swings, bloody nose, the porn addiction...Laura kept her head in the sand while John kept his in the powder.

Laura had three un-housebroken pugs who smelled like 15 kinds of putrefaction. They drained and deposited their canine foulness from one end of the house to another, and the whole inter-species family together was some kind of sight to be sure: John's transparent attempts to conceal his racing porno fantasies with a smile of domestic bliss which resulted in a tight-lipped death mask that would send small children running petrified for their fathers, as Laura, there with her skin-tight designer jeans, making one jabbing suggestion after another to John about honeymoon plans and reception logistics –and even children- all the while the stench of fresh urine, protein-rich excrement and the dogs' post-mortem halitosis would combine to engulf all five of them in the radiance of their own self-deception, desperation, and witlessness.

They would hold court, in John's richly furnished back patio, and that night his celebration for me was to include drinks at home *before* the bar, and a cookout with Dan and Tim in attendance. But the food never materialized, and I'd eaten a handful of John's Adderall, so that "celebration" concluded quickly with John ensconced in his room, and me in my curtain-annexed alcove with un-curtained floor-to-ceiling windows, both of us ready to ponder sex as a monolithic structure which we hogtied ourselves in the sub-basement of, all night long.

I passed out, from exhaustion and panic, around sunrise, laying sideways with my back flattened against the front wall of the alcove, underneath those massive bay windows where I was certain the whole state of Florida could see me.

After only an hour's sleep, I awoke to Sam's talons kneading my torso, and I rose to feed him downstairs in the kitchen. I could see that Tim was still up from the night before, through the back doors, a pair of French doors, where a broken washer leaked out onto the patio, rotting the wood, and where Sam's makeshift litterbox was stationed. Nocturnal Tim sneered at me through the side door of his adjoining garage kingdom as I stepped out onto the patio, then returned to playing the same 7 or 8 notes on his water-damaged grand piano. There, lashed high above the patio on a wooden privacy fence was a vinyl banner John had had printed for his failed line of gourmet meat seasoning: "Big Dick's Dry Rub" ("a treat for your meat! Just RUB it!"). Neither the patently offensive juvenile humor behind the product's name and slogans, nor its unimaginative components (salt, garlic, paprika, cayenne, cumin, lemon pepper...all the usual suspects) were sufficient for the entrepreneurial supernova John may have been anticipating. In a typically antiseptic, intellectually bankrupt manner, John was the kind of spoiled rotten manchild (from the Bay Area, of course) who believed that artists (and *all* people, most certainly) were as narcissistically motivated as he himself, the only d i f f e r e n c e being that someone like Tim, for example, was simply *born* with this elusive gift of *art*, which was obviously why John had *imported* penniless, disenchanted, and downtrodden old Tim from the West Coast: if tragic, wounded, devastated young John could not find his coveted "art", surely he could do worse than to fill his home with cutting edge poets and try his fledgling hand at the old novelty dry rub racket. The irony was that Tim was –if such a thing were possible- just as artless as John; in fact, given Tim's total and utter lack of work ethic, it stood to reason that John– given a time machine, and a smart reading list- could be Tim's superior in this regard as well.

I approached Dan then, on the back deck.

"Good morning, Dan," I said, softly.

"Oh hey Gene," he came back, in his tremulous, pack a day voice. He always sounded at once spooked and very bored.

Dan had a pronounced limp from Vietnam. He wore prescription Ray-Bans and didn't shave very neatly. A small man, a bit of a coward, a lackey, a drunk, a loafer. He *wore* loafers. Khaki shorts and a white-tee.

I liked Dan: my welfare card had not yet been issued so I'd been subsisting on his coffee and potatoes. Tim had warned me not to get into the habit of drinking beers with Dan so of course that's exactly what had begun to happen.

Dan needed a few more minutes with the morning paper, so I let Sam out onto the front porch to lay in the tambark. I tidied up my alcove, returning the sofa-bed to a sofa, witching off the Penthouse Channel on the plasma TV, and pocketing my new cellphone.

When I returned downstairs, Dan was waiting for me. We would hop the Central Avenue Trolley at Williams Park, about 10 blocks away, and ride it all the way out to St. Pete Beach.

I was wearing my biker boots with a pair of blue flowered trunks, a keepsake from my monstrous four days in Costa Rica with Izabela Slutzky. This was an ensemble which I believe I invented that day, and which of course I immediately fell in love with.

Dan and I entered a sinister convenience store called Stop-N-Go about halfway there. It was a real shithole, but bounding with tremendous life. A drunk old man sat just off to the side of the small parking lot, in a dirt yard, a sea of broken glass between a willow tree and a thousand year old industrial dumpster. I got the feeling that the man had been deputized, placed there in an official capacity by the store's owner, who turned out to be Turkish and a great pleasure to buy single cans of Budweiser from.

We placed our beers in my Alice pack (being a veteran, Dan was amused by my insistence upon this item, a lifelong auxiliary limb) and cut through Williams Park from the Northeast corner. Black junkies surrounded us with chants of "perks perks" and "party materials" and so on. Dan cursed under his breath; no country for old men. Bodies everywhere, and the general residue got into your skin and burrowed like a demonic spirit, a general vibe of coke and dope and bad skin, halitosis and body odor. Williams Park was itself, as they say of a drug casualty in Florida, "shot out". The park was one of two major hubs for the Pinellas Suncoast Transit Authority. It sat neatly not on, but AS one block of downtown St. Pete, and for me it loudly announced itself as a place where I'd be spending much of my time, one way or another. Buses lined up on three of the park's four sides, all of them with the blue and white PSTA logo, a wave. The dozen or so sheltered boarding areas, each with its own fiberglass encased display of maps and schedules, were teeming with bedraggled and dehumanized lower-class Floridians, or new arrivals like me, learning the ropes of the PSTA.

It was just a few minutes after 12 noon, a scorching and airless October day and on each of the park's corners was a Sabret hot dog cart.

Denizens of the 4th St. flops and other downtown flops chatted up the vendors, drinking Mountain Dew and smoking those "little cigars" or strolling through the park on narrow sidewalks that all connected in the center like the spokes of a wheel; the center was a marble fountain which had not been functional for a long time. The water sat stagnant and gone thick with pigeon shit. Some young black girls blew large blue bubbles in the Williams Park haze at the fountain's base.

"There's the trolley," Dan said, as I was reaching for my beer. We stood from our fresh squat in the grass, and watched it pull in. It was different from the other buses; it was yellow with a red roof, a trolley roof. The beach bus was a "fake trolley", and that sure did take the edge off all the grief of the park. A lot of money had been spent to transform the bus, you could tell, from a joyless inner-city behemoth into this cartoon thing. I half expected the driver to be dressed as a smiling dolphin, or a smiling crab. I thought of all those plush adult crab costume legs and antennae causing a horrific bus plunge when they got caught in the spokes of the steering wheel during a hard left turn, killing over 12 office-gossiping human beings in plastic chairs during their extended lunch break.

Dan said, "what the hell are you laughing about?"

But the bus door opened and the driver was just an ordinary fat lady in an ordinary PSTA uniform.

Dan and I boarded, paid, and began chatting about the beach as the driver smoked a cigarette where we had just been squatting. "Wow," I thought. "This is my new life. I am now a guy who can just hop a bus and go to the beach anytime he wants, which makes me the luckiest guy in the world."

Dan had been living with John for several years, here in St. Pete and elsewhere. I tried to imagine what could possibly have brought the two together, for they certainly disliked each other, and had absolutely nothing in common...but then again, neither did John and Tim. The three of them together in that house created an energy that was so thoroughly negative, I was surprised anything green actually grew in the yard. It was not simply unhealthy, not simply strange, but an indication, somehow, that something had gone wrong in the world, that something was amiss in the modern culture. Ultimately, I simply found it depressing. Within my first 48 hours I had correctly sized up the grim nature of the trio's warped dynamics. Three psychic cripples, all angry and terrified of themselves and each other. Lost, lost, lost.

John had the money, so that placed him directly at the center. John used Dan and Tim both as buffers between himself and reality, while the house there on 8th Ave. NE was a pressure cooker. I didn't want to be there when it blew.

The bus driver returned, circled around Williams Park,and we were headed west then: a straight line, Central Avenue, *all* the way west. ("The *OCEAN side, because it's not really the OCEAN, it's THE GULF*" I kept telling myself, because I pride myself on my navigational prowess.)

On the outskirts of downtown, the blocks seemed to grow longer, the traffic thinning out, the parking lots expanding in both size and atmosphere. I could feel a kind of psychic disturbance as we rolled past a hobo camp under an apocalyptic overpass. I considered once again St. Pete's most recent national attention as "the saddest city in America": for me, that would always be Harrisburg, and besides, sad or not, the ocean was the ocean –the *GULF, pardon me*- and Dan shook me out of these rabbiting thoughts.

"Relax, man, we'll be there in a minute."

I was taking flip phone photos of absolutely everything because everything caught my fancy: the smoked fish stand, the head shops, the donut shops, supermarkets, and the cheap motels: I was as giddy as a child on Christmas morning, expecting a simple beach which would have been good enough.

WELCOME TO ST. PETE BEACH

The handcarved wooden sign reading "Welcome to St. Pete Beach" greeted us as we hit the first bridge, taking us over the intra-coastal waterway with Pasadena, and the enormous Pasadena Palms hospital, fading behind us. Just to south, glimpses of Gulfport were possible.

I rose from my seat and began pacing, trying to capture every angle of every view, as if it would be 20 years until I'd be able to return. There was a second stretch of water, a second bridge, and the expanse of it all was like a solid right hook to my temple: all manner of watercraft and perverse blue of the afternoon sky...and the town unfolding now...St. Pete Beach Police Department, a large abstract white structure that resembled a military fortress, quite hideous...St. Pete Beach Hardware, also large and militaristic, and out of business...seafood restaurants, deep fried tourist fare, no doubt, throw a rock and you'll hit one...a supermarket called "Sweet Bay."

A chill ran through my body, all shivery delicious, when I tried to imagine doing my grocery shopping there at the "Sweet Bay". I was going to *live* here.

But the town was just beginning to reveal itself: a Christmas shop that stayed open all year round...a "XXX Supercenter" called "SHHHHHHHH!!!!!! Don't Tell Mama" right next door...I found that my mouth had gone dry and my hands shook.

"Jesus Christ, Gene," Dan chuckled. It's just a crummy little beach town."

The bus hit the main beach road, Gulf Boulevard, and made a right after one block, circling back around to the vicinity of the hardcore porn supercenter/Christmas-all–the-time shopping complex. We came to a rest by a bus shelter where a motley crew of drunk tourists and contemptuous old vagrants waited silently. The shelter was flanked by a large parking lot which served a broken down strip mall which had been sloppily renovated, maybe 15 years ago, and was now begging for renovation once again. That strip mall featured a snooty café and a decidedly un-snooty dive bar called Beach Lounge.

We de-boarded there; the bus would continue another 5 miles down Gulf Boulevard, but I don't think either of us were aware of that at the time. We made our way across the lot and past the strip mall, onto a side street which ran two blocks to the Gulf Of Mexico.

"Corey Avenue" led us through a small kingdom of dingy old rental properties to a cozy little beach bar concealed by ten foot potted palms: "Willy's Burgers And Booze". And beyond that, glimpsed as the mouth of a wide and treacherous looking inlet, was the Gulf itself.

"Ooooooh fuck!" I began jumping up and down and clapping my hands, stumbling like a mentally deficient child of eight on his first walk over hilly country.

Two Budweisers each at Willy's and we were off on a wander. The slum neighborhood gave way to an endless maze of cottages, bungalows, seasonal apartments, and monolithic waterfront condo complexes. It was at least 8 blocks until we found a proper beach access point which gave me the opportunity to be well and truly gobsmacked then: this was a horizon and a coastline, a grand scale spectacle, such as I had NEVER seen. I'd been waiting my entire fucking miserable wretch life for THIS.

The Northern Atlantic coast had a complacency, a melancholic defeatism about it; compared to this, the North Atlantic was in some way geriatric. It lended itself towards bittersweetness, mawkishness. Clam chowder and salt water taffy, crab cakes and clam bakes and beer and baseball and pony rides and Christmastime; *all* that stupid Northern shit.

This Gulf Coast out here, this was dangerous fucking business. This was the wild world; you couldn't be sentimental out here. Just *mental*, as in mentally ill, that seemed far more fitting for St. Pete Beach. I wanted to be savage and somewhere that *made* me savage; not in the sense of hurting someone, but in going into the night forever without caring how far I got…as long as it was *too far*. Far enough out there into that warm dark, and deep enough to wash it all away.

I was a little frightened, honestly. I knew I would never see my father again, for example. He died the following year. I knew it the minute I hit the water at a full run, Dan sucking down a Budweiser behind me, he himself like some kind of surrogate dad.

I would die here somehow and that was good and right and I welcomed it. I was happy with that. For the first time since childhood, I had discovered happiness.

Poor Dan had no one to talk to back there on the beach: I swam a mile out, and a mile back. I did this over and over again until the sun began to set.

I said very little on the way home.

It was possible now.

I forced it to make sense.

I would not let it go.

INTRA-COASTAL: VOLUME ONE

THIS SPORTING LIFE

Sunday was football day at John's. He gathered his lackeys – Laura, Dan, and Tim, and wired up a panel TV on the patio with booming Blaupunkts and a cooler full of Bud Light bottles. Maybe it was the Super Bowl that day. It always seemed like the Super Bowl to me when guys got together like that, even if it was baseball.

Everyone was in one degree of hangover or another: Dan's smoker's cough, Tim plodding about self-pityingly in a mangled pair of cargo shorts and a v-neck t-shirt with one sleeve missing, and then there was John, his feathery Aryan hair and drug-addled boyishness giving way frequently to queenie middle aged sarcasm...he had gathered his flock and we would certainly partake of his Bud Light except for precious, vulnerable Tim who pretended to regard us all insane for choosing to be up at the crack of noon. Normally, Tim did not rise until evening (John referred to him secretly as "Dracula") but John had turned one of the booming Blaupunkts about

30 degrees more than necessary away from the patio and towards the garage's side door, which was the only remaining access point to Dracula's lair now that Dracula had moved in and utilized the proper *garage door* as one of his walls. On it was hung a tattered poster for the 16 hour Fassbinder film *Berlin Alexanderplatz* which he told people was his favorite, although I don't think he'd ever seen it.

John told me that he was planning to have a hot tub

installed right in front of Tim's door, "so that Tim would

have to stay in there forever." He'd wasted no time confiding to me, and our loathing of besmirched, misunderstood Tim was our strongest bond. (Cocaine was the second, and I don't believe there ever really was a third.)

Shaggy old Jax padded out behind Tim as Laura arrived and Sam made a dash for the wicker sofa where I was sitting.

I lifted him to my center and deeply inhaled his fluffy coat: aside from the 4 walking stink bombs currently enjoying an afternoon Bacchanal of urination and defecation, Sam was happy there, and I was straining at my sales script.

"Hi, I'm Gene from Reece Builders, and we've been in the neighborhood this week putting in new windows for the McGoverns, and I just happened to notice that you're still using those old fashioned aluminum storm windows,

Yeah, it made me want to die, but it was the only way out. I read the lines back to myself a hundred, a thousand times, trying to stave off my shakes with that awful light beer.

I could never have imagined myself actually going down in this fashion: door to door, alcoholic, baffled and delirious, pathologically morose, willfully dysfunctional, and increasingly slovenly, making a fool of myself in strange doorways. I suppose if things got really ugly with one homeowner, I could simply bow out and find another house. Would people call the police on me? As a waiter, in a similar bind, I would not have that luxury, would I? As a waiter, you could be stuck with a table of asshole diners for several hours. In my case, it would be strictly rip and run, and I sought comfort in that: constant motion, no walls, no "team player" horseshit. The Florida sunshine.

The game went to "mid-inning", or "halftime", whatever it's called, intermission I guess, and John hooked up a DVD player, telling us he had something he wanted to show us. "Laura and I saw them live, and they were fucking amazing. They put on the best show in rock music."

He then produced a DVD, a concert film of The Killers, who I knew as a kind of glam rock stadium band. I was caught up in my script rehearsals until the thing started. The neighbors were grilling, I could smell their burgers and steaks; I hoped they liked The Killers because that's what they were getting, at a horrific volume. Sam bolted inside. John seethed with amphetamine profundity as the band tore into "Are We Human Or Are We Dancers" with a chorus line of nubiles, and sparks, and lasers, and I found myself trying to remember a nearly unlistenable Peter Laughner bootleg from the mid 70s, just before his death...Peter playing Richard Thompson and Lou Reed covers in a Cleveland barroom, probably 9 people attending, and it occurred to me that that may have been the last time things were any good at all, and that they would never get that good again. Lou, Richard, Peter...did these people not happen anymore? If not, then I may as well be in Florida, selling windows, taking buses to the beach, and jacking off to someone else's cable TV, in someone else's house. Fuck it.

I stood there in that perfectly nice house, with these perfectly unhappy and not-so-nice people, there on the staircase in the dark and I imagined it really always had been my curse to not just see the bad in everything, but like an auditor on an embezzling case, to see exactly where the bad started and finished, each strand of corruption and fraudulence, and it was dwarfing, that special lens of mine.

I switched on the TV, folded out the sofa bed, laid down, staring at people across the street having dinner and moving things around, being domestic.

I laid in bed the next day, all day, rising only to feed Sam. I'd work, I'd learn that script, and I'd save for a month. I'd find a small apartment on the beach. I'd build again.

STORM WINDOW TROOPER

On Monday morning, I rose at 6 A.M., staring at a purring, hungry Sam on the pull out couch as a penetrating, hallucinatory Tampa Bay sunrise attacked us fully through the bare windows. We basked in that light like zoo snakes, worshiping each other like that with the time that was left. Our road had been such an exceptionally merciless one and the guilt I felt for not having provided a secure, stable home (but rather a series of 35, 40, maybe 50 puerile homes) was enough to cripple me if I allowed it, along with all of the other guilt, acidic and violent guilt, unthinkable surges which I had been for so long using alcohol to conceal, to regulate, to endure. In the moment, I drank in the beauty of him, a minute, three minutes, then: "TREAT? TREAT…to EAT?" The pink nose in the air, the attempt to appear distracted, a little junkie pantomime.

We bounded down the stairs, got it sorted: coffee, eggs, potatoes. Sea Captain's Choice.

My lunch for Day One was two liverwurst sandwiches, potato chips, and a Snickers bar. I'd taken to buying cheap and unhealthy food until my welfare card was issued, then I'd be back to raw greens and blueberries and fresh lean meat. One more week, maybe two. I had a new headquarters to assemble, and a thing or two to show the mentally retarded Florida scum.

The 32 bus ran along the edge of Tampa Bay irregularly, but on that morning, it flung itself around the corner on Bay Drive right on time. I had my lunch in a thermal shoulder pack, wearing borrowed khaki shorts and a thermal top, a pair of slip- resistant kitchen shoes. The thermal was the only long sleeved shirt I had, and I knew it would murder me in the noonday heat, but I also knew my Frankenstein arms would kill any hope of a sale.

I hopped on the bus and snapped a few photos with my flip phone. With some difficulty, I found then that I was able to access the Internet with this device, logging into Facebook as the bus reached the commercial zone of 4th St. I fought off thoughts of that miserable turd who'd hired me, and exactly how insufferable he'd be the next time I arrived late. (As a pedestrian, depending on an undependable public transit system, some tardiness was inevitable.)

And as if the weekend had never even happened, as if my very skin was not still chilled with that first shock of Gulf water, I found myself walking that mile long avenue of spectral industrial blight, over Joe's Creek, and with that biker joint on the right, I opened the phone:

8:46 A.M. Perfect timing.

The office was neither cold nor quiet when I returned: the Maxwell House reek was in full bloom however, and there dashing around me was THE CREW. No one said hello, and I did not see fat Paul, so I helped myself to a cup of coffee and sat down in the room everyone seemed to be buzzing in and out of with their packed lunches and phones and cigarettes and cups of coffee. I shook hands then with several middle aged black men, each of them tall, bald, rail thin. They looked like felons. The a half dozen middle aged white men with pot bellies and glasses: definitely not felons, unless they were child molesters. And then two pretty but hopelessly trashy white girls with neck tattoos. I contemplated their stretch marks, knowing that I had found the bottom of the barrel once again.

I put my lunch bag in the fridge with the others, and sat down at a particle-board table as Paul finally emerged:

"everybody! SIT DOWN AND SHUT UP."

"Motherfucker," I could hear myself saying.

He glared at me, all intent underlined, gleefully:

"everyone say hello to JUSTIN!"

Mumbles and giggles.

"We are here today to turn this sinking ship around, m'kay? Last week...oh my fucking God, last week SUCKED! Worst week in...I don't know, I might have to check with Karen, but I think it was the worst week in the history of this company. Okay? New guy here, he's gonna do well, we got a hundred dollar van bonus authorized for today, solid leads...guys? COME ON! This is PITIFUL! GO GET SOME MORE COFFEE! DO SOME MORE METH! Whatever you guys did last week...well, whatever you DIDN'T do...because the week before that? It was great! I don't tell people how to live! Do it!"

There was murmuring and pained expressions, chuckles, winking, high fives.

"Do you know why you guys are gonna be bangin?"

More of the same.

"Do you KNOW why YOU GUYS ARE GONNA BE BANGIN?"

A collective "ooooooooooh".

"What?"

"Noooooooo!"

"BECAUSE YOU ARE GOING TO...Justin? Any idea? Tell us why WE GONNA BE BANGIN!"

"Because...we're gonna stick to the script?"

"BECAUSE WE'RE GONNA STICK TO THE MUTHA FUCKIN SCRIPT! And you've never worked sales? Sheeeeeee-it, this motherfucker right here gonna take the VAN BONUS! Listen people, THE SCRIPT WORKS. This is not A Night At the Improv, people. We use the script because THE SCRIPT works. Some of the shit I catch you people saying, and

Sharon, on the phones, when she's verifying, it just blows my mind. Just....the wackiest, dumbest fuckin' shit, and YOU ARE BLOWING IT, GUYS! You're just throwing money in the fucking trash when you start saying stupid shit. Don't be trying new things, don't be getting clever. STICK TO THE FUCKING SCRIPT. Let's rock. New Guy!"

Silence.

"JUSTIN! Come on, dude."

I stood up, rolling my eyes, "yes?"

"Pitch me."

"Oh for God's...really?"

"Pitch me. You want this fuckin job? Cuz you can fuck walk right now. I don't care. PITCH ME."

"Hi, I'm so sorry to bother you, I'm-"

"NO! Never apologize. PITCH ME."

"Hi there, how are you today? I'm Gene and I'm with Reece Builders, we're in the neighborhood today and, well, right down the street doing some work for the Reynolds and I thought-"

"NO. Vic, PITCH ME!"

Vic's bright mood, although he was 47 or 50, came from youthfulness, but no one else gave a shit. Lex said, "it be like this boss, you size the man up, and you don't put the nigger on the-"

"PITCH ME."

"Look man, I'm sorry to fuck with y'all but-"

Laughter.

"Mike, PITCH ME."

And so it went. A pep talk. No one was really expected to pitch anyone, but in your own private time, your perversity sold storm windows and they all knew, especially Paul, that there was no genuine formula for sales magic.

The biggest man, a black man, stood up and roared a fucking sermon. He was loud and gentle at once, and at once I knew he was the best salesman in the office.

Paul looked bored.

Paul was jealous.

"NATURAL, people. Let it be natural," he said, dismissing the black man. He said, "Alex makes more money than three of you put together. He makes more than I do, some weeks."

"Fuck you, fat man," I thought. "He makes more than you *EVERY* week."

"Alex makes more because he sticks to the script."

No one gave a shit. Their bright moods came from youthfulness, and if they were genuinely bright -but of course none of them were bright- then it came from the strain of that. You can't do well with intelligence in a world of apes. Just try it. You end up working against yourself. The sales floor, any sales floor, any sales ROOM, is about nerve, which is not to say good nerves or bad nerves, but nerviness, and that comes of course from bad nerves but you must never let that show. They'll eat you alive. You must eat yourself alive. That's sales. I knew that a long time ago, having had a salesman as a father: I remembered enough.

What Alex had was desperation. Prison had numbed him. Being black had numbed him. He was built for war, and he'd found Reece. He'd been locked up and in not wanting to go back, he invented a new magic. It made me sick to think about. I wanted what Alex had. I didn't have what it took to commit suicide.

The meeting was adjourned and the vans were loaded and there was cigarette smoke and more chatter. I looked useless. Felt useless.

"Krystal! Kelly! You're with me in van one. Justin, HERE. Everyone else, you're with Alex in van 2 or Dave in 3. Get the fuck out of here."

Paul tossed a cheap polyester sport shirt at me with the

company's generic logo embroidered on the right breast.

"You wear a large?" "Yeah."

"Put that on and get in the van. That's $20 out of your First check. Keep practicing your script."

"Okay."

"Oh, and I need your app. You didn't bring it, did you?"

"No, I'm-"

"Bring it tomorrow or your fired."

Three white mini-vans sat in the Reese parking lot, off to the side of the one story office structure. The black men –six- got into one van, the whites –four- got into a second, and in the third, it was me, the girls, Paul.

We were the training van, which made me wonder if any of us were eligible for the van bonus: the girls were borderline retarded, which meant they would probably do well in this job, but me, I knew how to make people laugh and like my old buddy Rockets –who killed Nancy Spungen- told me, if you make someone laugh, "you can get away with fucking murder."

Then again, I was becoming psychotically depressed, which probably wouldn't translate to comedy for the Big Mac slurping fuckholes of Seminole Heights, Florida.

I knew full well that once we hit the road, the radio would start blaring a song by Britney Spears or one of those people, and that Paul and the girls would start singing. I was exactly correct.

Around us was the most beautiful and haunting vegetation: the sheer decadence, the overwhelming natural vulgarity, the fecundity of Florida should make a truly LIVING man or woman, a thoughtful person, weak in the knees. But people are no longer awake in this country. They want grease, porno, death. They want industry. They want industrial strength poison, and they have no qualms about taking every last gator, every last muskrat, every last egret, every last dolphin, every last cat, every last great poet, straight to the big landfill in the sky with them.

Paul lit a Marlboro Light and began unfolding a map of the entire state of Florida as a torrential downpour exploded above us.

The temperature was already 90 degrees. The girls both had Burger King complexions with kinky brown hair that had been washed too many times with dollar store shampoo. They were talking about their "baby daddies" and jail time and Oxy and Roxy and shots of liquor; they would rule the earth. They overpopulated simply to dominate. I was looking straight at the end of the human world and there was nothing I could do about it.
Neither of them was old enough to drink or vote.
Paul wasted no time leaping into his passive aggressive "macho clown" persona, squealing in falsetto, "PARTY ALL THE TIME, PARTY ALL THE TIME!" as he steered the van out into the corporate chain badlands.

We finally came to rest a half hour later in a middle class suburb; it was a loop of ranch style houses, closed off from a kind of access road which opened to other loops, just as damp, and just as awful. The air was fetid, still after the cloudburst...everyone seemed to be sleeping or at work.

A mother duck waddled across the lawn of a brown ranch house with trash strewn all over its porch and the barking of a vicious dog inside could be heard through the thick but battered front door. The duck's 10 or 14 ducklings waddled behind it. The girls noticed this and said nothing whatsoever about it.

"Okay," said Paul, lighting another cigarette. "We do not approach every house. What houses do we approach, Krystal?"

"The ones with the old-style windows?"

"Aluminum windows! We sell vinyl hurricane-proof windows! Capable of withstanding 100 mile an hour winds! If they have aluminum windows, they're fucked! 'We are in the neighborhood'...LISTEN! You guys need to know this, you're supposed to have this down! 'We are in the neighborhood installing new windows for your neighbors the Richardsons, and-'"

"I've been saying 'the Blackstones', I don't know why, isn't that a cartoon?"

"Krystal, shut your pie hole. Listen. 'We're only here another day so we're letting you know that we have a special offer this month, and you can-"

"I thought Maviano was good, that's my sister's boyfriend's name, the new one."

"Oh for Christ's sake Kelly, the name doesn't matter. You have a list of fake names right there if you need it, just relax and be natural. Pick a name you're comfortable with, and stick to the script."

Paul reached into the van and pulled out 3 clipboards, then handed them around. "Justin, follow me. Girls, you two stick together. I'll see where you are in half an hour. Good luck. Let's sell."

For the next 30 minutes, I stood limply and listlessly on one red brick or concrete front porch or another, one after another, a thousand lizards darting over every inch of each one, over and across left-out children's toys, slimy with moisture and white trash neglect, burger grease and excrement, tropical cockroaches mostly just out of sight, 30 dogs howling in unison, as Paul turned on the smarm to beat the band. I was astounded at his porcine pathology, and even moreso at how many people warmed to him. Both parties, most shocking of all, seemed to be enjoying themselves. No one, of course, was interested in new windows, which were probably unreliable and non-durable anyhow. Paul would prattle on and on; the homeowner standing there enraptured – not by Paul's salesmanship, but by the strange, anomalous intrusion itself- for up to 10 minutes: "we've been in business for 62 years, and this is a family owned company. All of our windows are made in Allentown, Pennsylvania, and we have an 'A+' rating with the Better Business Bureau. Also....no? Well, a little something to think about further down the road then?" Rubber banded to my clipboard was a thick stack of full-color brochures to leave with an unconvinced homeowner, or pinched in the screen door if no one answered.

It was slow, hard going and I began wracking my brain for other possibilities, drawing a fresh blank with each panicked inquiry. Within the hour, we'd all reunited with the girls for lunch, and we were all sweatsoaked.

"Any luck?", Paul said brightly. The girls stood there in silence, looking helpless, trying to find a reason to giggle so they could return to their somnambulant chatter about anal sex and karaoke.

"Come on," Paul said. "Lunch, and then new hood."

After an inspiring siesta at a combination Pizza Hut/Taco Bell which was surrounded by yellow tape from an under-renovation shopping center, Paul opened his map, chanting "rock and roll, party all the time, rock and roll, party all the time", made some large Xs with a pink high lighter pen, then gunned the engine.

"I'm gonna keep us all together for the rest of the day. You're not getting it. We haven't had ONE sale. I want you to watch what *I* do. COME ON! Rock and ROLL! Partay all the tahm, partay all tha tahm, mad money mad money, who's your papa,, who's your papa?"

As he roared out into a six late highway, we were nearly t-boned by a Coors Light delivery truck. "Learn to fuckin drive!", Paul bellowed. My heart sank when I opened my eyes to find myself still alive and holding that clipboard. My fingers were sticky with taco sauce and I silently belched up half my toxic lunch, then swallowed it back down again. We must have walked 30 miles that day, shadowing this pornographic retard every step of the way. He sold nothing of course, and of course, this was the girls' fault, and mine.

When the 32 bus found me back at Industrial Road, I could not bend my legs. I could not think or walk or speak. I boarded the bus, sat down, pulled out my flip phone, and looked at it. I couldn't figure out what it was.

Sam was waiting for me in the rock garden back in the Old Northeast. He resented even the shortest separation and so did I. We were outnumbered; plain and simple.

I stayed up until 4 A.M. drinking water and trying to memorize the script from start to finish, and also the procedure which I had a greater difficulty with: that included an awkward cellphone interaction with the homeowner, a lot of paperwork, a lot of back and forth. Beyond that was Paul...I simply could not take another 9 hours of that motherfucker. How had someone not stabbed him to death? Had me made his parents suicidal? What monsters must they be to have created him?

In the morning, I discovered that my food card had arrived the previous day and so I hotfooted it all the way downtown −a 23 minute run− to Publix where I picked up a ribeye steak, a dozen eggs, my *own* coffee, and a box of Emergen-C.   (The vitamin packets were not covered by the Florida welfare administration, so I crushed the box and shoved it down the front of my jeans.) I'd scarcely returned before it was time to run for my bus to Industrial Drive. I slapped together a bag lunch of candy bars and processed meat; I pocketed 2 of the Emergen-C packets (these would save me my soul to keep) and took off at top speed, just catching the 32.

Sam was out of Fancy Feast. I needed to make it as a window salesman.

INTRA-COASTAL: VOLUME ONE

THE POSSIBILITY OF AN ALLIGATOR

Back in the van with the girls, I did not quite hear Paul's vile snickering and bellowing. I heard only the script. I did not see the parking lots zipping by, or all the chain link, the dismal special offers. I saw doorbells and welcome mats, oceans of them. I saw mouths moving and then smiling, I heard laughter and lies and I heard ocean waves crashing around me.

I saw St. Pete Beach.

"You're awful quiet back there, Justin."

"I'm getting ready for war, Paul."

"Mmmmm-kaaaaay. Cray-cray!"

The radio returned. It all sounded the same, bombastic bubbleheads...Paul and girls began mouthing every word, in some kind of trance.

"The beach," I thought. "The beach, the beach, the beach."

By lunch, it had happened. I was stuttering, I was losing it, but I'd set my first appointment for a home demonstration of REECE storm windows. Paul let me go off on my own then. He had no idea, still has no idea, how close he'd come to getting slaughtered.

I pulled out my *cellie*, clipboard in hand, and dialed the office.

"Terry, this is Gene, I'm here with a...ah, Mr. Mark Ziegler? Okay, sir?"

I would then hand my sweat soaked gadget to the increasingly skeptical robe-wearing rube and occupy myself with imaginary notations on my clipboard as one of the phone reps buttered the man up, while running a credit check on his blind ass, pure jackals they were...and then he'd hand the phone back to me and I'd be clued in: "deadbeat", or "he's a go."

A date would be set then, the form would be introduced and completed, and I'd be on my way. This process could take anywhere from 10 to 20 minutes.

We covered 8 different neighborhoods in as many hours. Every house had at least a dozen dogs, which all screamed in unison, screaming like they were being tortured to death. They hated their miserable lives too.

I completed 4 appointment forms that day, having been face to face with nearly a thousand strangers.

Maybe it was Largo, maybe Seminole, maybe it was Indian Rocks Beach. I never knew where we were, which meant that there was always the *possibility* that the ocean lapped at the shores somewhere just to my right or my left and I liked that. I liked that very much.

The territory hardly mattered; it was all outer space to me.

On the third day, I began taking alcohol to work with me, little bottles of Crystal Palace and Mohawk vodka, and then there was this terrible syrup called *Dragon X*, which claimed to be "orange wine". The citrus odor seemed to mask the alcohol. I never became drunk –not once- but simply loose, and I was always quick to remind myself that this was the first job of my life –that I could remember, it may bear admitting- that offered me some form of profit sharing, if I needed encouragement beyond the booze and the weather.

My father was a veteran salesman and I wasted no time calling him up to boast of this new development in my life.

He said, "oh yeah yeah, that's GREAT, buddy."

My dad.

He'd been sick and tired of my stinking ass for too many

years. I was in bed then, but after we hung up I went to CVS and bought two four-packs of Schlitz Bull Ice.

On the fourth day, I was livid to discover that only 2 of my 4 appointments had made it to the sales board. During my time at Reece, that sales board would become a malignant fixation, the fixation that drives all salesmen, that drives the moral disintegration and decay of *people* though *salesmanship*.

It was explained to me that it is not unusual for the prospective client to change his mind and cancel, sometimes within seconds of the arranged product demonstration. More frequently, they would simply refuse to answer the door when the representative arrived.

(I never discovered the particulars of the demonstration, but I liked to imagine hungover divorcees jumping up and down on slabs of fiberglass and knocking over ceramics on mantles while wildly gesturing Category Three gusters with their trackmarked arms in the cramped living rooms of old people and common young suburban breeder slobs whose husbands drove trucks for Pepsi-Cola . I never saw, much less met, an actual representative of Reece, and I didn't know what location they worked out of, but for some reason, I'd decided they were all devastated heroin addicts. And drunks. The whole thing stunk to high heaven.)

As for my two dropped sales, I found it more than likely that either favoritism, head-tripping, or stone-cold thieving were far more likely explanations. What could I do but take my lousy 50 bucks and keep showing up? I considered something I'd heard on The Wire: "you can't lose if you don't play."

But if I was going to be truly honest, I had to come to terms with the fact that pushing windows for a corrupt sales firm was far less brutalizing than the racist abuse and swamp rot Hell of washing dishes for P.F. Chang's, or Ruby Tuesday.

I attempted a means of getting myself off on the voyeuristic aspect of Reece's door to door routine, but the suburban squalor, the routes themselves, were so thoroughly dampening –beyond rumors of alligator sightings, or ocean fantasies- as to disallow, outright, the possibility of any aberrant romanticism. It was simply bleak, the constant dog barking, the endless rainy highways. I instead drifted to thoughts of the desperation and agony and rage of Aileen Wuoronos, or any of Florida's millions of displaced road casualties. But it wasn't the place, not this place, just as so many of the perceived L.A. problems I had 15 years back had not always really been L.A. problems, and the NYC problems were not necessarily NYC problems...it was the age, the post-literary age...I was a true freak, one of the last, a man stripped of all traces of irony, and I would have had problems anywhere.

I'd have to learn a new way. This undercover routine, well...I was not fooling anyone. They would allow me in, on default, and out of pity...and then they would simply ride me to death.

Reece paid each Friday, which was such a blessing I could have wept. That meant beach money. It meant a sliding scale membership at the YMCA whose sauna I required to rid myself of all that cheap alcohol, so as to be "freshly squeezed", to have that light and airy "clean" feeling. My body was very much becoming rotten with alcohol, my mind nearly cooked with worry and fear. I scored a record breaking 7 appointments that Friday, and my euphoria lit up the van during our return to St. Pete. I screamed at Paul, "rock and ROLL! Party all the time, Paul!"

I prayed that come Saturday morning, the board would register at least 5 of them. I cashed my check at Wal-Mart that evening 3 miles west, in a crack and heroin ruined no-zone which would prove integral to my beach dream.

ROUTINE 666

St. Pete is a small peninsula on the western side of the big peninsula known as Florida.

Central Avenue begins in downtown St. Pete, exactly at the edge of that stagnant old Tampa Bay, and runs a straight line west across that little peninsula St. Pete all the way out to that golden Gulf of Mexico. You can bike the 10 mile distance in about an hour or less, depending on your choice of bicycle. Without a bike, you hop the trolley bus for $2 or ride all day for 5.

Central, east of 25th Street North, is all hipsters and yuppies; not a fucking soul among them, trust me. Not one. There are chi-chi art galleries, micro-breweries, thrift stores. It's devoid of interest to anyone who's ever lived in a REAL city, unless they're stranded in St. Pete and pining away for their own putrid bohemianism back home. Cunts.

Otherwise, the real St. Pete doesn't emerge until you hit 34th Street North. There is no 34th Street South, unless you count the driveway of the YMCA.

The St. Pete YMCA is a 40 million dollar complex, and it sits there spookily on 7 acres of land; it is about the general size and shape of a southern plantation. Built in 1989, by the Felcher family, who I am certain are ourtright ghouls, the decidedly un-Christian YMCA is to my mind the saccharine sacred heart of St. Petersburg.

The blackened lungs are right across the street: on Central Avenue, between 33rd and 34th Streets, between the YMCA and the barometric death clouds of 20 crack motels, stands Central Station. It's a *saturating* social experience, to put it mildly; a structural eyesore and a resounding testament to the systematic efficiency and inexorable scumminess of inner-city public transportation hubs everywhere. Central is, essentially, the equivalent of a Greyhound terminal, say Cleveland's, or Philadelphia's, on Christmas day, with its walls, roof, janitors, and security force all swiftly eliminated as if they had never been there at all. It says more about St. Petersburg, and indeed the whole Tampa Bay experience, than anything else you will find here. There are so many routes, so many buses, that you sit down, crack a beer, fresh off a Greyhound from Dogpatch, and you get to know St. Pete pretty goddamned fast. The size of it, the people, the energy, the soul of St. Pete is Central fucking Station. The PSTA erected this column of high-functioning lunacy in 1987: built of solid glass blocks with concrete reinforcement, the main circular body of Central Station is about the size of a baseball diamond and resembles at a distance a kind of synthetic, futuristic mockery of Stonehenge, or a derelict space station, a merry-go-round for 15 foot humanoids. Rising 40 feet, that center column is used as a ticketing office: there is bullet proof glass and public bathrooms you know better than to use unless you're about to mess yourself (syringes and blood spray, etc).

There are 42 steel benches and 26 slanted boarding areas for the neverending influx of road-weary behemoths whose arrival times are usually displayed on newly installed LED monitors which hang from the monolithic station's crumbling dome ceiling. By and large, the PSTA runs a pretty tight ship, and each riding experience is determined by the temperament of the driver. I am very much in love with two of them, a white girl and a black girl; we exchange emails and I imagine having a bus driver girlfriend would make me the most bad ass motherfucker who ever lived, and I tell them that. "You trouble, boy," the black girl says, giggling.

The white one wants me to go to rehab.

Central, until around 9 p.m., will be teeming with waiting travelers, every one of them, to a man, to a woman, bearing the telltale signs of attrition, of neglect and self-neglect, of an entire life lived in the wake of some form of sexual abuse, below the poverty line, and off the radar. Nearly everyone you meet there is a heavy smoker, and after 20 years as a portal to work and home for untold millions of these people, Central Station could easily be said to be the world's largest ashtray.

I found the place in equal measure heartbreaking and wonderful. "At least I'm moving", that's how I dealt with it...a Johnny Thunders lyric. No one liked where they were going, but they were going. It was life. It was Big Metaphor.

I circled it several times, struggling for geographical footing. I wanted a place of my own, first of all: a place I'd never run into Jim or anyone else I knew. No hideous yuppies whom I had to pretend to like when I went out with John. And here I was, exactly halfway between North and South, between St. Pete city and St. Pete Beach. The junkies surrounded me, grinding it out. There was a dirty old tropical Wal-Mart there too, and I decided I would buy the things I needed for the beach there. I would need a machete, and a fishing rod...an umbrella...dish soap...I would heal there. I would do my fucking shopping there.

I was halfway home.

I returned to 8th Avenue with a membership to the YMCA and my Army pack stuffed with a hundred pounds of groceries: a real mover and shaker in this world. It was evening and the 15 minute walk from Williams Park to the house had fairly destroyed my back; I heaved and sweated and loped and weaved around like a drunk, cursing that load when Sam leapt from his hiding place in the yard and greeted me, silently as ever. An enraged Tim was laying in wait also:

"Geeeeeeeeeeeeeeeene, maaaaaaaaaaan.....this is not working ouuuuuuuuuut, we need to tallllllllllllllk...."

"Tim," I said, "I worked all day and I have a hundred pounds on my back, can you give me five fuckin minutes please?"

"Nooooooooo, maaaaaaaa, lisssssssten to me...."

"Tim," I said again, stepping past him into the house, "I gotta take these groceries off my back."

He followed me into the kitchen. Sam, sensing Tim's necrotic force field, held back.

I put the pack on the floor, undid the top.

"This is not what we agreeeeeeeeeed to, Geeeeeeeeeeeene....fucking dishhhhhhes in the sink this morning, two dishhhhhhhes, I know they were yourrrrrrs, Geeeeeeeeene maaaaaan, not cooooool..."

"Tim, I was running late for work, I am sorry. I'll be more careful, okay? Look, I'm *hungry*, man, please? Will you let me put these things away and eat?"

"I'm gonna have a talk with Johhhhhhhhhn maaaaan, you gotta gooooooooooooooo..."

"Tim, I am moving out very soon, and for now, I am busting my ass."

"Fuck you mannnn, I work harder than annnnybody. You gotta go nowwwwwwwwww."

"Tim, I will sit down and talk with John tomorrow."

"Fucking ASSSSSS hole..I knew this was a mis-taaaaaaaaaake."

Whispering rodentine Tim vanished then through the French doors.

Later that night, after I'd enjoyed a ten dollar bottle of Tempranillo and that forsaken ribeye with roast potoatoes and a Caesar salad, I retired upstairs with Sam. Dan, sensing the tension earlier, had barricaded himself in his own closet sized room and was playing solitaire on his computer. I was drifting towards sleep when Tim drew back the hallway curtain and invited me down to the patio to smoke a joint. For the sake of harmony, I put Sam aside, leaving him to pout in the dark, and followed Tim down the stairs.

I'd been given "the tour" of Tim's garage space during my first week there – a queen sized bed and a barge-sized desk dominated...there was also a baby grand piano which Tim thought he could play. A few thousand books on mounted shelves and several 6-foot bookcases. Quite a cozy little arrangement, it had to be said, for which Tim had not paid –and would never pay- a single dime.

I sat down on the bed and braced myself for another lecture, awash in something which I had for so many years defined specifically as "Ramirez-dread". The man was simply insidious.

Bypassing all that toxic energy, Tim spoke of the weed he'd just bought from a dwarf, a New York dwarf who worked as a doorman at a local club. Tim knew I was beyond tired and that encouraged him. He knew I wasn't a weed smoker. I hate the shit. But he had no other means of asserting his power. I allowed it, I told myself, for Sam's sake.

Tim tried talking about Nelson Algren, insisting that *he* had introduced me to the iconic, brilliant writer.

"No Tim, that was Delbert Yates who gave me my first Algren book."

"Noooo, maaaaaan...that was meeeeeee. You're so ungraaaaateful, Gene. I've GIVEN you so muchhhhhh and you don't even knooooow, maaaaaan."

"Goddammit motherfucker, I got up at 5 in the fuckin A.M. and I am not gonna sit here with YOU and bicker about who turned who onto what."

Tim got up and pulled a stack of books off one of his shelves, then dropped the stack in my lap. I looked down: trade paperbacks, full color covers. Tim's "arts and culture review", *Esoteric Babies*.

"Look, maaan…I put all of those together in one *yearrrrrrrrr*, man. I *worrrrrrrk*. That's my *worrrrrrrk*, Gene."

"How many did you sell?"

"No, mannnnnnn, you don't *gehhhhhht* it!"

Issues 1-5 of *Esoteric Babies* had come out looking sharp, if altogether uninspired. I leafed through them muttering the obligatory compliments. He had simply acted as a compiler of mostly low-rent transgressive/ underground babble/psychosis in the form of comic strips, photos, amateur journalism, and incoherent writing. He was once again attempting to trade on the talent and energy of others, that much was patently obvious. Just as obvious to me was Tim's complete and utter lack of marketing acumen –or work ethic in general. He'd been *busy*, certainly, but the magazine was a wholly fraudulent enterprise: unfocused, undiscerning, and ineffectual. I couldn't imagine that he'd been able to put more than 20 copies of each into circulation.

"Here, Geeeeeene," Tim snapped, while pointing to the cover of issue #3 which was a photo of a beautiful woman with a footlong cock. "That was my tribute to you. You're into that whole tranny thing. Don't deny it. It's not cool to be in the closet in 2011, dude."

"Good night Tim," I said.

"No, duuuude, wait a minute, don't be a DICK. I want you to be in the new issssssue."

"I want nothing to do with subculture anymore. I'm done. It's nothing but a filthy sandbox for retarded babies. Retarded ESOTERIC babies."

"You diiiiiiiiiiiick," he grinned. "This is why you've never been successful, you're just a fucking SHITHEAD to everyone."

"See you tomorrow Tim." I went back into the house.

That cover, I have to say, was pretty fucking hot.

INTRA-COASTAL
VOLUME TWO
WILL BE PUBLISHED IN
*****SPRING 2015*****
BY MONASTRELL BOOKS.